THE REBELS
1.5, The Breeder Files

About the Author

Eliza Green tried her hand at fashion designing, massage, painting, and even ghost hunting, before finding her love of writing. She often wonders if her desire to change the ending of a particular glittery vampire story steered her in that direction (it did). After earning her degree in marketing, Eliza went on to work in everything but marketing, but swears she uses it in everyday life, or so she tells her bank manager.

Born and raised in Dublin, Ireland, she lives there with her sci-fi loving, evil genius best friend. When not working on her next amazing science fiction adventure, you can find her reading, indulging in new food at an amazing restaurant or simply singing along to something with a half decent beat.

For a list of all available books, check out:

www.elizagreenbooks.com/books

BOOK 1.5 IN THE BREEDER FILES

THE REBELS

ELIZA GREEN

Copyright © 2017-2020 Eliza Green

The moral right of the author has been asserted in accordance with the Copyright, Designs and Patents Act 1988.
All rights reserved. No part of this publication may be reproduced, stored in a retrieval system, or transmitted, in any form or by any means, without the prior written permission of the author, nor be otherwise circulated in any form of binding or cover other than that in which it is published and without a similar condition being imposed on the subsequent purchaser.
All characters in this publication are fictitious and any resemblance to real persons, living or dead, is purely coincidental.

ISBN: 9781098532246

Copy Editor: Andrew Lowe
Proofreader: Rachel Small
2020 Update: Nerd Girl Edits

Cover: Deranged Doctor Design

*Dedicated to those who enjoy one-dimensional characters.
Don't read this.
You won't like it.*

DOM PAVESI

The Rebels

1

A loud crunching sound filled the atrium. Dom Pavesi jerked his mop to a stop. Screams from the other participants bounced off the walls. He sucked in a hard breath and lifted his gaze from the floor to the scene before him. Two fallers. He'd overheard conversations about the suicides from those who'd already rotated.

Others with dilated eyes hurried to get mops and buckets. Dom gripped the handle of his mop, turning his knuckles milky white. He had no similar Compliance buffer to protect him from the horror, no interest in following whatever rules Essention and Arcis demanded.

The shutters squealed up, and a nose appeared from the inky-black cave where the wolves lived. Dom straightened up, huffed out his tension and wheeled his bucket of water over to where the fallers had landed.

Ω

The bell for the end of shift rang. Dom stretched out his lower back, sore from hauling the fallers from the floor to stretchers. He didn't mind hard work, but why did the wolves need him and the other participants to clean the damn floor?

The Rebels

The only constant he could rely on these days was the number of steps it took him to get anywhere.

One, two, three, four.

Five steps from Charlie's front door to the street.

One hundred from there to the end of the street.

Three hundred from the end of the street to the first factory.

Only two hundred to the scanner positioned high on the wire that ran the width of the street. Its beam was broad and quick. Dom had tried weaving through the back of the factory out of its path, but it always caught him out no matter what route he took.

The running track behind the small bungalows in West Essention and the playground were the only areas the scanners didn't reach. The area had once belonged to a town called Annavale. Charlie said it was likely the machines had built the urbano around it.

Dom counted the steps from the force field surrounding Arcis to the base of the Monorail platform. He couldn't see a use for his counting yet. But then, the controllers of Arcis and the urbano didn't know rebels lived among them.

The train took him a few stops, to the east of the urbano, where the orphans had been assigned accommodation. The doors opened and he stepped out along with most of the passengers. This urbano gave him the creeps. No curfew. No police presence. Which meant the controllers must be watching them in other ways.

He descended the stairs from the Monorail platform to street level.

Exactly fifteen steps.

Seventy-eight steps from street to home.

His and Sheila's temporary prison in East Essention was a single unit on the top floor of a row of grey accommodation blocks. He approached his block with three doors to the front, set on different levels. An old man passed him, grazing his fingers against his forehead in a lazy greeting. To keep up the pretence, Dom reciprocated with a similar greeting.

Fifteen steps from the street outside his apartment block to the first door.

Thirty more steps above that to his front door.

He stared at the cold, grey metal and lifted his wrist containing a chip to the plate. One of the doctors—or nurses—had given it to him. He'd been too sick to notice who and when. He and Sheila had been soaked in sweat and dry heaving into a bucket in Foxrush when the people from the city of Praesidium had come for them. The radiation poisoning had been the rebels' plan all along. But it hadn't been easy to live with the sickness.

Like some damn miracle, the doctors at Essention's hospital had reversed the effects of ionising radiation. Dom had relayed his concern to Max and Charlie about how fast they'd nullified their plan. But Max had said the plan all along was to get rebels inside Essention, which they'd done.

He sucked in a deep breath and released it. A little unease was nothing compared to losing his mother. Mariella had entered this urbano—and presumably Arcis—never to return. That happened four months before the radiation attack.

The door clicked open and he pushed against it. Music assaulted him the second he stepped into the hall.

He slammed the door closed and dropped his backpack on the floor. 'Sheila!'

They were supposed to be blending in.

The music was coming from her bedroom. He marched to it and found her lying on her bed, eyes closed.

She smiled as her head bobbed along to the beat.

'Sheila!'

Her eyes flicked open. She flashed him a wide grin and patted the area beside her. 'Come join me, Dom.'

He strode over to the music player and speaker set by the bed—items she had brought with her from Foxrush. He hit a switch on the side and the music disappeared.

'We're supposed to be blending in, not making a racket. What if Essention sends someone to check?'

Sheila sat up. 'What happened to the impulsive imp I knew and loved from Foxrush? The one who would take a stray dog home and feed it, then let it run wild around the house. Remember when you did that? Your mum was livid. And the wet dog smell!' She gagged. 'Or the one who used to break into Mrs Lewis' house when she was out so he could play her piano. Man, those were good times.'

Dom stared down at her.

'What happened to him, Dom? You're like Mr Control in here. It's like you've become my parent.'

'Have you forgotten why we're here, Sheila? Or are you more interested in acting like a stupid kid?'

She pulled Dom down onto the bed and sat cross-legged, facing him. 'I remember. But I've been in this apartment for a week now and I have literally *nothing* to do. If I was on Compliance, then maybe I wouldn't care as much. There's not even a drop of alcohol in this... this freaking prison.'

Sheila had arrived in Essention the same time as him but had been too sick to join Arcis at the time. He'd had three weeks before her release to comb over the place for bugs and cameras. Max and Charlie believed the units and houses weren't being monitored because of Compliance.

'I know you've been bored around here, but I expect you not to get into trouble.' He scrubbed her scalp with his knuckles.

Sheila jerked her head away. 'There's the teasing sonovabitch I became friends with.' She leaned forward and hugged him briefly. 'Welcome home, loser. How was your day? Anything exciting happen?'

He shivered as he remembered the fallers.

'Fine. And no. It's pretty dull in there.'

'I can't wait to start tomorrow.'

The wolves had said that rotation was imminent. One of the boys on the ground floor, Ash, who'd been passed over for rotation, had said new recruits only joined once per rotation.

'Out with the old, in with the new,' Ash had said.

Dom's mind flashed to the image of the dead bodies. He couldn't figure Ash out.

Sheila eyed him curiously. He picked her up off the bed and set her on her feet. 'If it helps, I missed not having you around. It's been pretty shit around here. Lonely and shit for three weeks.'

That was the truth. Alone, his mind had replayed too many events he couldn't control. That's why he counted the steps that never changed.

'What can we do about it?' Her finger grazed the side of her music player. She lifted a brow at him.

Dom sighed. 'Okay, but quieter please. We don't need anyone checking on us.'

'Yes, boss.' She turned on the music and lowered the volume.

He liked the music. It gave a sense of normality to the place.

'You hungry?' he said, walking from the room.

Sheila snagged his wrist and turned him back to face

her. 'Hungry for you, lover.'

She pulled him to her chest. At five feet nine, she was almost the same height as him. 'You want something, Sheila?'

She traced her finger down the side of his face. 'How about you show me some of your moves?'

Dom's lips twitched. 'You sure? I'm pretty bad.'

'Yeah, give it to me.'

He pushed her away and twirled her once before gathering her to his chest. He dipped her low, drawing a little whoop, then brought her back up. They moved a little slower. 'Like that?'

'Yeah. Just like old times. You know that drove Kaylie wild when you danced with me.'

Kaylie was a girl they both knew from Foxrush. Dom had a brief fling with her before coming to Essention.

'I don't really notice what others are doing when I'm dancing with my girl.'

Sheila pouted. 'Dom, you say the sweetest things.'

He jerked away. 'Now I know you're definitely on Compliance. You're being too nice.'

'I'm just remembering one night, one close night between you and Kaylie. That's all.' She paused, her finger on her lips. 'Wait... Wasn't there another girl? Mia?'

Dom tugged the band out of his hair and let his dreadlocks spill around his olive-skinned face. 'You make it sound like I was hopping around everyone.'

'All the girls wished you were. They told me.'

He cocked a brow.

'Okay, maybe not to my face. But I know girls better than you do. Trust me when I say this, Dom Juan. You weren't short of a few admirers in Foxrush.'

Dom didn't like where this conversation was

headed. He turned to leave. 'Come on. I'll make you something to eat.'

Sheila followed him to the kitchen. 'You miss your girls at home?'

'I'm sure they're doing fine without me.'

Mia and Kaylie had joined the rebels and were working out of a compound hidden in a mountain range. It was one of a few safe havens, unknown to Praesidium. Truth was he hadn't thought much about either of them, not since his mother had disappeared. 'Besides, I've got my hands full with you.'

'Yeah, I guess you do.' She leaned against the door frame. 'Although, I'm sure they'd scratch my eyes out if they learned what we get up to all alone in this house.'

'What? Dancing?'

She winked at him. 'Among other things, lover.'

Dom shook his head. Sheila loved to flirt, to be dramatic. She was also funny, sharp-tongued and one of the bravest girls he'd ever known. But it would never be like *that* between them.

'I think it's time you left this apartment. You're starting to hallucinate,' said Dom. 'Looking forward to starting in Arcis tomorrow?'

Sheila shook her head and laughed. 'Hell, no. It sounds terribly boring. But it beats waiting here for my man to come home to me every night.'

2

There was a nervous vibe in the air. Or maybe it was just Dom who was feeling nervous. Rotation was due—the wolves had practically guaranteed it with their speech yesterday. Ash said they showed up more frequently when announcement was imminent.

Inside the busy atrium, Dom wheeled his bucket of dirty water over to one of the cleaning vestibules.

One, two, three. Ten steps from his section to the vestibule.

He tipped his water down the chute and stored his bucket away.

A noise caught his attention. He turned to see the four wolves hassling one of the boys. The boy's face had turned bright red in their presence.

The atrium had three solid walls and a glass wall, the latter which faced North Essention and the water purification pipes. One of the solid walls had a door and a shutter that concealed the wolves' living area. A door in the second solid wall, where the garbage chutes were, led out to the lobby.

Exactly thirty-one steps from where he stood to the exit.

Three mounted cameras were perched halfway up the third solid wall above the cleaning vestibules. The cameras were attached to steel girders. Except for Dom, none of the participants appeared to have noticed them. He knew the precise location of the blind spots, in particular one that gave him a good, unobstructed view of the first floor.

The squeaking sound of metal claws on tile set Dom's teeth on edge. The wolves continued to weave in and out of mopping workers. Dom found himself standing taller and more alert in their presence. He hated the clean-freak beasts. He had yet to figure out their purpose here, or what their orders were.

One, two, three... Eight paw-lengths from the shutter to where the wolves often gathered in front of the cleaning sections. Twenty-eight steps for Dom.

The lead wolf growled at the group.

'Participants, line up. Rotation is imminent.'

The others dropped their mops, including Dom. He studied the wolves' feet as he slipped into line, wondering how fast they could move on the white-tiled floor if he were to attack one.

Rotation was guaranteed, Max had said. And Ash had been here one rotation too long. He was standing casually in his spot, arms folded and eyes on the floor. Ash looked around him, catching Dom's eye. He gave him a tight nod and looked ahead of him.

Neither Max nor Charlie knew what the programme was really for. But what they did know was that anyone who had entered never came out.

Dom clenched and unclenched his hands. The thought of venturing deeper into a place with no way out made his hands sweat. But Sheila would be joining soon. He would make his time on the first floor count. And at lunch, they could discuss its layout and strategise.

He counted twenty-three other participants. He knew none of them except for Ash, but only because he'd been more vocal than the rest.

The wolf/machine hybrid continued. 'The following people have made it to the next floor.'

Dom listened to the six names. None were his.

His heart sank.

'Please follow me to the elevator,' said the wolf. 'Everyone else, back to work.'

Three boys whooped loudly and three girls gave a little screech. They chatted as they followed the wolf out of the room. Ash, one of the successful candidates, went with them. He shrugged at Dom and said, 'Maybe next time, hey.'

Dom ignored him and stared at the remaining wolves retreating to their dark cave, too shocked to count their footsteps.

His chest felt heavy, like one of the wolves was sitting on it. He'd done everything asked of him. How had he missed rotation? What had he done differently from the others? Why had he been passed over?

Swearing softly, he tugged on his dreadlocks until it hurt.

The others returned to their duties without a word of complaint. Sometimes he wished he were on Compliance, to be stuck in its dreamy haze, to be carefree like they were. All the antidote did was to show him how unfair rotation was. He'd put on the same act, to appear like everyone else. So why hadn't he been picked?

Dom glanced up at the cameras and pulled himself together fast. Max and Charlie would be livid when they heard about this.

Two girls loitered at one of the cleaning vestibules

as they discussed rotation.

'I can't believe I didn't make it. I was so sure I would.'

The other girl giggled. 'God, now I'm dying to know what's on the first floor.' She turned and noticed Dom standing there, waiting for her to move from the vestibule.

'Excuse me,' he said to her.

She smiled and touched her hair. 'Sure.'

The girls did that a lot. Smiled, fixed their hair when he approached, acted friendly to each other, to him. Maybe that's why he hadn't been rotated; he was too closed off to the idea of making fake friends in this place.

Dom pulled out a bucket and mop and thanked the girl. A blush stained her cheeks and her gaze dropped to the floor. The girls reminded him too much of Mia and Kaylie back home. He walked away and started on his section.

The door to the lobby opened and the wolf who had left with the rotated six returned with twelve new people.

Out with the old, in with the new.

Sheila entered the room and he sighed with relief. She was staring at him.

The last wolf returned to the open cave and the shutter squealed as it closed. All the new participants stood waiting for instructions except for Sheila, who walked over to Dom and punched him in the arm.

'I didn't expect to see you here. What the hell happened?'

He rubbed the pain away. 'I don't know. Only six people were rotated.'

Sheila glanced around the room. The boys stared at her. Her beauty—perfect skin, tanned, long golden-brown hair—could be as powerful as Compliance at times.

'We'll talk about that later,' said Sheila, smiling sweetly at a group of boys. They blushed and looked away. She turned back to him. 'How about you show me what crappy work I've got to look forward to?'

Sheila knew how to act—unlike him. But he'd made a promise to Max and Charlie. To his mother, even though she didn't know it. Dom fixed his expression until he was sure he looked as vague as the others did.

Dom showed Sheila the ropes, while the others who hadn't been rotated explained it to the rest of the newbies.

One of the new girls caught his eye. She had shoulder-length brown hair and looked to be around seventeen years old. Her eyes delicately roamed the space. Her rounded shoulders and hands shoved deep in the pockets of her uniform made her look smaller than she was. She seemed timid, afraid. Unsure. One of the boys bounded over to her and she shrank back from him. He smiled at her, asked her name. She relaxed her shoulders a little.

Dom saw her lips move, but didn't catch what she said.

Ω

An hour into the afternoon's shift, Sheila was lagging behind the others. She leaned on the top of her mop and huffed, 'Is this it? I was really hoping for something a little less mop and a little more watching movies.'

Dom smiled. 'Sorry, no movies. This is pretty much it for this floor.'

Sheila looked around. Her gaze stopped on a group of girls by the vestibule whispering and glancing around.

She perked up. 'Well, that looks interesting. I always did like a gossipy bunch of girls. How about I do some recon?' She used her mop to steer her bucket over to the vestibule and introduced herself. The girls, wary at first, seemed to show more interest in Sheila when she pointed to Dom.

They laughed at something and Dom tried to tune in to their conversation. Sheila worked fast; she'd been in Arcis just an hour and was already making friends. He ignored her and ran a clean mop over his section. He would ask her later how she put people at ease so quickly.

Sheila remained at the vestibule for a while, chatting, laughing, and pretending to be girly. An act for the cameras, no doubt. A shiver caught him when he thought about someone watching their every move. He put his mop away and turned to the camera's blind spot, the only place where he could breathe. He froze when he saw someone was in it.

The girl with the brown hair and blue eyes—the timid one who'd been here for half a second—had stolen it. Heat bloomed in his chest as he strode over to her. How dare she steal the only thing in this place worth a damn? She probably didn't even know what she'd found.

Her brows tugged forward while she ate an apple and stared at the ground. Dom's approach startled her and she looked up at him. But she didn't leave. Instead, she shuffled to the side, and dropped her gaze to the floor again.

Dom huffed out air through clenched teeth and settled beside her.

He felt her tense up at his proximity. That became more obvious when she shuffled again to make room. Or to get away from him; he had that effect on some people. The girl continued to eat her apple.

Dom rested his hands on the railing behind him. His plan was to stand here long enough to make her uncomfortable. But he was the one feeling out of place. He couldn't tell her to leave. A blind spot in the camera's view needed protecting, and he couldn't risk her blabbing to the wolves about it.

He glanced at the girl. She wasn't like the others: chatty, friendly, hopelessly under Compliance's spell. This girl was quiet, meek and thinking a hundred things. And he wanted to know what those things were.

Maybe he should try this friendship thing. Get on Arcis' good side. Secure rotation.

He turned to her. 'Hi, I'm Dom.'

The girl looked up at him. He drew in a tight breath when he noticed her eyes: rich, blue and sad, despite her dilated pupils.

Her gaze shifted back to the ground.

Dom elbowed her lightly. 'This is the point where you tell me yours.'

'Anya,' she said, almost as if she hated the name.

'So how's your first day going?'

She shrugged, the tension in her rounded shoulders never lifting. What horrors must she have faced on the outside to still feel strong emotions while on Compliance? He waited for an answer other than a shrug. She looked up at the first floor.

His discomfort had him clenching his fists again.

Screw it. Making fake friends went against his nature. He would stick with Sheila. They could play it up together for the cameras.

He prepared to walk away, to give up on this girl, when she said, 'Did you know this is the only spot in the atrium where the cameras can't see you?'

His heart stilled at her words. He couldn't help but laugh. 'Yeah, actually. I was about to tell you to go somewhere else.'

She locked eyes with him. 'So why didn't you?'

'Because you looked like you needed a moment.'

She nodded. Bit her lip. Put the rest of her apple in her pocket. 'Thanks for letting me have it.'

She pushed away from the railing and walked back to her section. His gaze followed her, and for the first time he noticed she was in the section beside his.

Dom's heart beat too fast. He glanced up at the empty floors above him, shook off the feeling and returned to work.

3

After their shift in Arcis had ended, Dom and Sheila headed over to Max and Charlie's house in Southwest Essention. With the freedom to come and go, they used every available moment to discuss strategies. Max predicted it would be only a matter of time before Arcis changed the rules.

Max stood by the fireplace in the living room, his arm draped over the black mantel, scrolling through data on a small screen. Charlie, his seventy-year-old father, sat on the sofa, glasses perched on the end of his nose. He held up a small, square metal piece to the light.

Their first introduction to Max and Charlie had been Foxrush. Long before the radiation attack on the town, both men had turned up and rounded up the townspeople. Their questions about Essention had struck Dom as a little odd, but when Max suggested the urbano had something to do with his mother's disappearance, he started to pay attention. That's when he learned about the rebels.

At first, Dom had trusted the pair about as much as he had his asshole father, Carlo. There was only one person who he trusted to have his back. When Billy Swanson yanked up nine-year-old Dom's T-shirt to get a better look at his scars, Sheila Kouris had jabbed at his nose with her fist. Billy had cried for days and never came near Dom again. He and Sheila had never spoken about it.

Now, in the living room of some long gone family, Dom watched father and son, at ease in each other's company. His jealousy flared; his own family structure had been questionable. Mariella had done her best to raise him right. And whenever his father got the chance, he'd strip Dom of all those lessons and push him back down.

Because of that, Dom killed him.

Charlie looked up first. His weathered face broke into a smile when he saw Sheila. 'Come here, my girl!' He patted the space beside him. 'I never get to see you much these days.'

Sheila dropped into the seat and gave him a hug.

If anyone trusted people less than Dom did, it was Sheila. But seeing how easily she accepted Max and Charlie made him rethink his own trust issues.

Charlie kissed her cheek.

She giggled. 'Charlie, why don't you ever drop by our little prison block? We can serve you meat and stale bread for dinner. A meat-crap sandwich.'

Charlie hushed her. 'I won't have you making fun of the food from our factory. All handmade by me and Max, you know.'

Sheila picked up one of his hands and turned it over to examine it. She brought it to her nose and sniffed. 'Hmm. Oil, grease, metal.' She let it go. 'I bet you don't even know how to make a pie.'

The old man laughed. 'I missed you, darlin', and that sharp tongue of yours. I wish others had the guts to speak their mind like you do.' He cupped her face, the piece of metal still pinched between his fingers. 'I just wish you'd say what's in your heart. We all love you.'

Sheila squirmed. Charlie let go of her face and dropped a kiss on her head.

Her mask was back up. 'No flirting, Charlie. Dom's gonna get jealous. Isn't that right, Dom?' Still by the door, Dom smiled. Her eyes glittered with mischief, but he saw the effort it took for her to keep her mask up.

'That's right.' Dom stepped closer. 'Sheila's *my* girl.'

Charlie put his hands up, feigning resignation. He winked at Sheila and she nudged him lightly.

'If you're hungry, you can get something from the kitchen,' said Max.

Charlie stood up with a grunt. 'Let me get it.' He put the metal piece down on the table and left the room.

'Thanks for putting a smile on my dad's face,' said Max to Sheila. 'It helps him to forget.'

'Well, it just so happens I'm not faking it.'

Max, Charlie, Dom and Sheila had arrived in the urbano together after the people from Praesidium had found them all in Foxrush. So far, their familiarity with each other in Essention hadn't raised any suspicions.

Dom followed Charlie to the kitchen. The old man took down four bowls and a couple of cans of potted meat. 'It's nothing fancy, but it keeps us from starving.'

Dom laid out the bowls on the table, opened the cans and began scooping out the contents.

Charlie leaned against the counter, his light-blue watery gaze fixed on Dom. 'You seem quiet. What's up?'

'I missed rotation.'

He considered telling him about the suicides. But what good would it do?

Charlie nodded once, short, sharp—exactly the way Carlo used to nod, right before...

He shook off the memory with a shiver. He wasn't

back there with a man used to getting his own way. This was Charlie. Charlie and his father were nothing alike.

'It's okay,' the old man said. 'You'll rotate next time. It's not like we're going anywhere. We're prepared to see this out for as long as necessary. To get answers.'

Dom sighed and scooped meat out into the bowls. 'Yeah, I know.'

'Well, what's troubling you?'

He hadn't told anyone about his past, about how certain quiet moments stirred deep, restless feelings within him. 'Nothing. I just don't like being kept back. I thought I'd be further along by now.'

'This is new territory for all of us. We don't know what's going on in Arcis, so don't put it all on yourself. I've seen you do that before. Shoulder the blame for what happened to your mother, take on the responsibility of others. Sheila, for one. She can handle herself.' Charlie squeezed Dom's shoulder. 'Why not let her carry some of the weight?'

Dom looked up at Charlie, his spoon halfway inside the metal can. He wondered what man he would have become if he'd had a different father. Charlie had lost someone, too: his wife, to the stress of losing a child years earlier—Max's younger brother. Both Charlie and Max were open about their life before Foxrush and Essention. That unsettled him, people knowing secrets and intimate details about him. Sheila was the only one to know what really happened. He trusted her to take that secret to her grave.

Dom thinned his lips and resumed scooping.

'Did I ever tell you what I used to do in Halforth?' Charlie said. 'Before Max and I took up with the rebels?'

Dom shook his head.

'I used to be a barber.'

'Really?' That surprised him. He scraped the remaining contents out of one can.

Charlie laughed. 'Don't sound so shocked.' He pointed at Dom. 'You have impressive hair, boy. And while I would never encourage you to cut your dreadlocks, if you ever fancy a change, know that your hair couldn't be in better hands.'

Dom touched the snarls of hair that hung just below his neckline. 'I don't know why I kept it,' he lied. 'It's the easiest and the hardest hair to maintain.' He laughed once. 'I've actually forgotten what I look like with short hair.'

Charlie studied him. 'It's like your armour, a link to your past.' His words unsettled Dom and he stared at the old man. 'Don't be angry, son. I've been a barber for nearly thirty-five years and I've gotten pretty good at reading people. I see how some folks get when their hair is cut off. Might as well be losing a limb in some cases. Many don't want to let go of their old selves. So they come in, ask for the exact same cut. Safe. Then there are the ones who don't struggle with the decision. They're carefree, bold, happy to show the world they aren't afraid of a little change. And then there's you.'

Dom frowned.

'You're one of the people on the edge. You want to change, but you're stuck inside your own skin, tied to a past that is not of your making. Your dreadlocks show the world that you're different, but you're also masking something deeper. An indecisiveness that keeps you from trusting others.'

His breath caught in his throat. It was like Charlie was looking into his soul. He thought he'd been hiding his secrets well enough.

He locked the fear back inside and flashed a smile. 'And you got all of that from my hair?'

Charlie watched him some more, then shook his head. 'People tell me I should have been a psychologist. I read people better than a shrink ever could. And I'm cheaper too. No more than the price of a haircut.' He nodded to the door. 'Take Sheila out there. She's a sweet girl. But she hides her secrets like you. I like her. She's tough.'

'Yeah, she is. She likes you and Max and she doesn't say that about many people. Trust me.'

'And I like you both. Believe me, I don't say that lightly, either.'

Charlie grabbed a wooden board with a loaf of bread on it. He took a bread knife and one of the bowls and carried everything into the living room. Dom followed with the remaining three bowls.

Charlie had almost cracked his secret. The thought of people he respected knowing he was a killer made him sick to his stomach.

They placed everything down on the coffee table. Sheila was holding up the tiny square piece of metal.

'What's this, Charlie?'

He wagged a finger at the object. 'I'll let my son explain.'

Sheila put it back and grabbed some food.

Max picked up one of the bowls and a wedge of bread. He used the bread like a spoon and took a bite. 'First, tell me what happened at rotation.'

The image of the suicides the day before haunted him.

'Not much to say, except I didn't make it,' said Dom. 'Only six did.'

'Out of twenty-three?' Max rubbed his stubbly chin. 'I was sure the programme was a ruse, that all the participants would rotate, no matter what. So Arcis is being picky all of a sudden? Now I want to know why.' He shook the piece of bread at Dom. 'What's your impression of rotation? What's its purpose?'

'I don't know. I think Arcis expects something from us.' He didn't know what. 'A reaction, maybe? Everyone who's on Compliance is acting like a robot. How can you expect to breed individuality in an environment like that?'

'You two are the exceptions.'

'And yet, they didn't rotate me.' His thoughts flicked over to Anya and how she wasn't like the others, even on Compliance.

'Go on,' said Max with a nod. 'First impressions, please.'

Dom chewed on his thumb—a nervous habit from his days of dealing with an unpredictable bully of a father. He hooked his thumb in his belt loop instead. 'The work is bullshit. The wolves are an oddity I can't figure out. The facility is supposed to teach us how to become adults. I don't know, maybe we need to start behaving like adults, or something.' He sighed. 'I can't help feeling like I was kept back because I didn't blend in enough.'

'So it's predictable?'

He wouldn't say that. 'Except for...'

'What?' said Max.

'The suicides.'

Sheila's eyes widened. 'Why didn't you tell me?'

'I didn't want to scare you.' Truth was talking about it reminded him of his father and what Dom had done to him. All he wanted was to forget about that man. No chance of that happening any time soon.

'Suicides?' said Max. 'Where did they come from? When?'

All eyes were on him. He rubbed a hand over his hair. 'The day before rotation. Two fallers. All I know is they came from above.'

Max began pacing. 'All the more reason for you two to make rotation next time.' He stopped pacing. 'Dom, I want you to remember why the others rotated. Make friends. Use their experiences to blend in.'

Sheila swallowed a mouthful of food. 'If it's a friend you need to become, Dom, then a friend I can teach you to be.' She lifted her brows at Max. 'The girls are practically salivating over this one, but do you think he even notices?'

'I'm not interested in taking advantage of drugged-up girls, Sheila.'

'I'm not asking you to. Just flirt with them a little. Make them feel special.' She batted her eyelids at him. 'The way you make me feel all the time. It's not hard. Just start by opening your mouth and saying a few words like, "Hi, my name is Dork."'

Dom glared at Sheila. She stuck her tongue out at him.

Neither Charlie nor Max laughed. 'We need you to immerse yourself in the programme, Dom,' said Max. 'We need you to reach the ticking heart of Arcis. The ninth floor. Have they said anything to you about why they didn't rotate everyone?'

Dom shook his head. 'The wolves watch, supervise. Then they go away.'

'At some point, we have to assume you will be forced to stay in Arcis. It's what happened to others.' Max held out his hand to Charlie. He picked up the tiny piece of metal and dropped it into his palm. 'Charlie has come up with this device—so you can stay in touch.'

He handed it to Dom.

'It's a communication card made of an inert metal. Pretty rudimentary. Responds to a series of taps, like

Morse code. You know the basics, right?'

Dom nodded. He'd learned them while doing tactical training with the rebels.

'How do I wear it?'

Charlie tapped the area behind his ear. 'A small incision. It will just look like a small scar. Sorry. We can't risk them finding it on your person.'

What was one more scar? 'That's fine.'

'Just the one?' said Sheila.

I have two. It took me a long time to find enough inert metal to make them. We only need one point of contact. Sheila, you'll act as Dom's backup.'

Sheila tossed her mane of hair back. 'I'll pass. I prefer my skin unblemished.' Dom stared at her, and her face drained of colour. *Sorry*, she mouthed.

Dom shook his head with a look that said not to worry. He had to accept sooner or later that his scars were a part of him.

'It's not an option. Both of you need to wear them. Max and I must insist,' said Charlie. 'If something happens to either of you, we need to know.'

Sheila snorted. 'Fine.'

Dom stood up. 'I'm going to use the track outside before I head home. Can I get the key?'

'Sure,' said Charlie. 'Let me insert the device first and test it before you go.'

Dom turned to Sheila. 'You want to come running with me?'

Sheila laughed. 'And ruin this perfectly shaped body? Hell, no!'

4

Apart from the sound of mops swishing across the white-tiled floor, there was no noise inside the atrium. A few days had passed since rotation and the buzz from the new participants had been replaced by monotonous repetition. Busy workers crammed into the open space that felt more claustrophobic since the suicides.

Dom craved the outside, especially the ache in his legs when he ran. Running helped to clear his mind a little. He just wished he could use the track more often. But Max warned him not to develop any patterned behaviour.

He checked the time, groaning when he realised there was still an eight-hour day ahead of him. It wasn't a long track, maybe a few kilometres in a straight path, running behind the bungalows in West Essention. He would run in one direction, then turn and run back. After a few laps, he usually ended up in the empty playground past one gated exit. He'd lie on the grass for a while and remember the piano at home, the one his mother had bought from a neighbour. It was an old upright and nothing special to look at—some of the keys were missing —but Dom loved the sound it made. His mother adored music even more than Dom did. He'd learned to play in

Covington, a town five kilometres west of Foxrush.

Music had started out as a distraction, for him and his mother. Dom hated fighting, but he'd made an exception for his father. Carlo had despised his piano playing so much he'd broken three of Dom's fingers—two on one hand, one on the other—slamming the lid down while Dom was practising. It had been the longest six weeks of his life.

But his asshole of a father was no longer breathing. Dom had made sure of it.

The wolves, alert and roaming, snapped him out of his thoughts. He dragged his mop across his section and waited for them to leave, which they usually did, eventually. They liked to watch the participants. Perhaps to unsettle them? He had no idea what was going through their minds, or if the part-machine-part-organic beasts were even capable of independent thought. Twenty minutes was their maximum length of stay, but they usually gave up after ten. Dom saw no pattern to the exact amount of time they stayed on the atrium floor. The only certainty was they showed up at least once a day.

Dom caught Sheila looking at him. She stuck her tongue out at him. He smiled back at his bolder, braver friend. She'd already made several new friends. The younger boys followed her around like she was a goddess. The older boys played it cool around her, talking louder when she was near. The girls regarded her with wariness, while others happily chatted because of the attention she brought with her.

Sheila stuck with the girls mostly. She'd never been comfortable around guys, always resorting to snippy comments to put them off her. Dom had been her safety net for as long as he could remember.

But there was one girl who kept her distance from

everyone; one who mopped alone and ate alone. One who drew his attention every single time.

Anya stopped and rested her arm on the top of her mop. She dragged her bottom lip through her teeth while the wolves continued to roam. Her casual stance sent a prickle down his spine. He stiffened when one wolf turned and examined her with its yellow eyes. She stared into space, like she was in a daydream or something.

He hissed a curse through his teeth, irritated by her blatant disregard for the rules.

Without knowing the wolves' motives, they must be feared. Given the right circumstances or motivation, they could turn on everyone.

The wolf continued to watch her. Anya's gaze wandered around the atrium.

What the hell is she doing?

Her ignorance made his hands shake. The others weren't aware of what was going on. Sheila was too busy blending in to notice the girl.

He sucked in a mouthful of air and released it. He needed to snap her out of it.

It's none of your business what she does, Pavesi.

So why did his heart hammer whenever the wolf got closer to her? It sniffed the air between them, as though it were trying to work her out. And yet Anya, leaning on her mop and caught up in her thoughts, showed no reaction. It was almost as if she were inviting the attention.

The image of the suicides flickered in his mind.

He mopped closer to her section. The loud roar of his heart thundered in his ears. He tried to catch her eye just as the wolf inched closer to Anya, more curious now.

He nudged her arm with the handle of his mop. She jerked and blinked at him in surprise. Her eyes were dark-blue pools of confusion.

Dom nodded at the wolf. 'You've got company.'

She turned to look and blushed. As if she'd been woken from a dream, she mopped her section hard, glancing up at all four wolves that were now lined up before her. Her fear shook the mop, impeding her progress and earning her a growl from one wolf.

He wanted to stand in front of the girl, to block the wolves' access to her, to take her punishment for her like he had for his mother. But he was supposed to be indifferent to this behaviour, to pretend he was drugged.

Anya turned sharply and dunked her mop in the bucket of water. Water splashed everywhere. One of the wolves jumped back from the liquid. He saw her chest rise and fall too fast. She kept her eyes on the floor and concentrated on her section.

The four of them dispersed suddenly and roamed the atrium separately. Dom watched the girl as she looked up, looked around. Her fingers fluttered at her throat. Dom swallowed down the hard knot in his.

$$\Omega$$

Lunchtime came around and Dom couldn't wait to escape the tension. Sheila was distracted with her new female buddies. But he didn't mind—Sheila chattered too much and he needed time to think. He grabbed some food and found a secluded spot outside. Dropping to the grass, he pressed his back up against the wall. The sandwich, made in Max and Charlie's factory, felt dense between his fingers. He took a bite, grimacing at the sweet taste from the medication that no longer kept him in a stupor.

Anya walked outside and sat cross-legged on the grass a few feet away, staring at the food she'd brought with her.

Changing his mind about alone time, he collected his things and walked over to her.

'Is this seat taken?'

Anya looked up at him in surprise as he sat down, not waiting for an answer. He usually gave strangers a wide berth, but something drew him to this girl.

'I just came outside for some air,' she said quietly.

'Me, too.'

They both sat in silence. Dom chewed slowly, running through conversation topics in his head. Anya unwrapped her sandwich and took the smallest of bites. She barely looked at him. He wasn't good at reading people. Did she even want him there?

Anya wasn't like the other girls in Arcis. Compliance made them all the same. They laughed, smiled, and tried to get more of his attention. But this girl didn't care if he stayed or went.

He remembered when he'd met Kaylie a year ago. They'd gone to the same school but he'd barely noticed her until she started talking to Sheila. She'd been coy about talking to him, glancing over at him, expecting him to make the first move. So he had, because girls wanted guys to do the work. Kaylie had laughed at his lame jokes and played with her hair. And after, Sheila had slapped him on the back and told him she was renaming him Dom Juan because he was clearly so smooth with the ladies.

But when Kaylie had wanted to take things further, he'd panicked. He didn't want her asking about his scars.

The laughing, the joking, the flirting: it was all fake. He didn't feel like someone to be desired. But with Anya, he sensed that if he put on a show, she would see right through it. See him for the fraud he was. And that unnerved him.

He stared at his legs.

Anya remained oblivious to his presence. He admitted to liking the silence. Just being in another's company was sometimes enough. But he also admitted to liking her voice and the things she had to say.

He sneaked a peek at her; she caught him looking. Her brow was furrowed, as if she was trying to work him out. What assumptions had she made about him? What conclusions had she reached? Would she guess what he was? A rebel? A killer?

'Where did you come from?' she said.

Her innocent question widened his eyes. He pulled his surprise back fast. 'From one of the towns. You?'

She tilted her head to the side. 'You don't look like the other boys here.'

I haven't been a boy for a long time.

Dom tugged on one of his dreadlocks and smiled. 'Yeah, I guess not.' He wondered how well his fake smiles masked his secret: that he was too old for the programme and a rebel. That he'd grown his hair out on purpose because Carlo hated long hair on boys. Dom had inherited his father's looks—coffee-coloured skin and slim nose—but at least he could control his hair.

If Praesidium had done its job, then Anya and the others would believe the rebels were the enemy. Max had warned him and Sheila never to reveal who they were to anyone. The rebels were hated, despised. And Compliance made Praesidium's lie much easier to swallow.

Anya stared at him for a moment too long, then dropped her gaze back to her food. She took another tiny bite. Dom wondered if the Compliance had curbed her appetite.

'Why aren't you inside hanging out with the girls?' said Dom.

She shrugged. 'I like it out here. It's less crowded. I

guess this is going to sound a little bitchy, but the girls in there aren't really people I could be friends with.'

Dom smiled to himself. Another thing they had in common.

'Am I on that list of people you can't be friends with?'

Anya looked up at him; the sincerity in her eyes forced him to swallow hard. 'I don't know you well enough to say.'

Dom shifted so he was front of her. 'Okay, ask me something. Just to put your mind at ease.'

Anya abandoned her food and made a bridge with her fingers. 'Okay, do you work out?'

'You mean with weights and stuff?'

She nodded.

'Yeah, I do.'

'Why?'

He frowned at her. 'Why do people normally work out?'

'There are a number of reasons, but two I will mention. Because they're vain or they use exercise as an outlet for something.'

Dom leaned back on his hands, his legs still crossed. 'Well, I guess I'd have to say the latter.'

Anya nodded and frowned at the same time, as if she was making new assumptions.

'Do you?' He'd noticed her lean and strong body.

'Not since I came here. I used to run in the evenings but that all stopped when...' She took a deep breath.

Dom almost blurted out about the existence of the running track.

Maybe she'd find it on her own.

'I like the way running makes me feel,' said Anya. 'Alive.'

'Yeah, the weights keep me strong. And I like to run, too. It clears my head.'

'Exactly!' She smiled, and Dom saw her true beauty. 'I sleep really well after a run, like my mind is empty enough to switch off.'

'So, the girls in here aren't potential friends?'

'Nah. I'm sure they're nice and all, but I'm not interested in the same stuff they are. It's easier for me to be alone.'

'But wouldn't it be easier if you made friends? Make the time a little less painful?'

She laughed, and it was the most thrilling sound. 'Like you do? I've seen you, Dom Pavesi. All alone at lunch. Never talking to anyone all day.'

He lifted a brow. 'I'm talking to you, aren't I?'

'Yeah, but before that. You have a routine. You don't stray from it.'

'You're watching that close, huh?' His voice shook with nerves. He hated being predictable. But in Arcis, it was expected. And essential.

Anya blushed so hard he wanted to touch the burn. 'No, I just notice things, that's all.'

Was he becoming easy to read? He'd have to be more careful around her, to not wear his own secrets like a jacket. His heart slammed against his ribs as he asked, 'Yeah? And what have you figured out about me?'

She examined her fingers, losing interest. 'Not much. We all have secrets. Sometimes it's best not to ask.'

Dom wondered what secrets she carried around.

The bell sounded and Anya jumped to her feet. She gathered up her lunch and walked back without waiting for Dom. He watched her leave.

Why did this girl fascinate him so much?

5

Dom waited for Sheila by the entrance to Arcis after their shift. The early evening sun was beginning to dip in the sky, but not by much. It was moving into summer and there was a small stretch in the evenings.

Sheila sulked as she approached with her backpack over one shoulder. He guessed her mood had everything to do with Arcis.

Dom counted, but Sheila's stomping and sighs as they walked shot his concentration to hell. He shook his head to dislodge the interruption and started over, adding the missed steps to his count. None of it was necessary—he knew the exact number from the entrance to the force field around the perimeter of Arcis. But the task kept his mind off other things, like the real reason for the programme.

Exactly twenty-two steps from entrance to edge. Same as that morning.

Dom slipped through the thick, heavy, humming force field, made easy with the chip in his wrist. Once he'd tried going through the force field using one of Charlie's discs, a generic one that worked to block the signal. He'd positioned it over the chip, as Charlie had instructed him to do. With the signal blocker in place, the field became denser and more resistant against his body. When he removed the blocker, the load lightened instantly. The only explanation he had was that the chip in his wrist must sync to the frequency of the force field.

Max had tried to pass with his general chip, but the force field stung him. Only the teens coming to Arcis could pass, and that worried Dom.

It meant he and Sheila were on their own in Arcis.

Another reason why he counted.

Sheila said nothing all the way to the Monorail platform. He saw Anya a short distance ahead of them, holding on to her backpack like it held some treasure. She wore the Essention uniform—black trousers and coffee-coloured tunic. Strands of her brown hair had come loose from her ponytail and the gentle evening breeze made them dance. She stared ahead of her. The only thing eye level this high up was the wall surrounding Essention and the guns that pointed out.

When other girls neared Anya, she shrank into herself. Dom wanted to warn her that being an outcast guaranteed you nothing in Arcis. To rotate, she had to play the game. After one missed rotation, Dom was beginning to realise that friendships and allies mattered—not just to guarantee rotation, but also to Arcis. Ash had been the most talkative of the bunch and he'd rotated along with five others, who'd also made the effort to be friendly.

He and Sheila boarded the train and sat together.

Sheila huffed out a breath. 'I'm so sick of this. I hate manual labour.' She held her hands out and examined her nails. 'Look at my hands, Dom. They're ruined.'

But Dom was only half-listening to her. He watched the participants around them smile and nod at things being said. But then they slipped into a glassy-eyed Compliance stupor, like they drifted in and out of awareness. Dom knew what the drug felt like to be on. Before receiving the antidote, Max had insisted he and Sheila experience it, to know how to act like the others.

It had been the worst couple of days of his life. His mind had not been his own. A deep fog had invaded his clearer thoughts that kept him from counting, kept him from seeing things he would have noticed in an instant.

Like the menace of the wolves.

On Compliance, they were hazy, soft versions of themselves. Not really there, not really a threat. Off Compliance, the outlines of their bodies sharpened into focus and their unnaturally yellow eyes simmered with obvious restrained violence. It frightened Dom to think how fast he'd accepted everything while on the drug.

They arrived back at their apartment block. Sheila dropped her backpack on the hall floor, kicked off her shoes and padded barefoot into the kitchen. Dom followed. She pressed onto her toes and pulled out a can of beans from one of the cupboards.

Her nose wrinkled as she held up the can. 'I wish there was something else to eat.'

She swept her hair over one shoulder exposing her tanned skin. She was beautiful and any guy's dream girl. He'd known Sheila since she was eight and he was nine.

Holding the can, she turned to him. 'You know what I want to do right now?'

She had that look in her eye. The one that usually killed his appetite. 'What?'

'I really want to raid the factory for something other than goddamn beans. You think Max and Charlie would mind?'

'Under different circumstances, I'd say no.' Dom rubbed his neck. 'But we're supposed to stay here.'

He was sick of telling her they needed to keep a low profile. Even though he hadn't found evidence in their apartment of bugging devices or cameras, the mere existence of this urbano bothered him. He kept any chats about rebel matters cryptic, including why he and Sheila were really in Arcis.

Just to be safe, he blocked the doorway. Sheila watched him for a moment before rolling her eyes and huffing.

With a grunt, she emptied the contents of the can into a pot and turned on the heat. 'Okay, I won't go anywhere. For now. But I can't say what I'll do tomorrow, Dominic. And you can't watch me all the time.'

'But I can lock you in your room.'

She lifted her eyebrows and looked at him slowly. 'Kinky. If you're in there with me.'

'Sorry, that doesn't work on me, Sheila.'

She bit her lip suggestively. 'Are you sure?'

Dom ran his hand across the back of his neck. He hated it when she played her games.

To get off topic, he walked over to the table and cut the stale loaf there into chunks. Next, he got two bowls and Sheila dished out the hot beans evenly. At least the beans were high in protein and would fill them up.

They carried their food into the living room; Dom hated the sterile kitchen. Even though the entire unit had a similar feel and look, at least the arm chairs in the living room were comfortable. He sat in one while Sheila settled on the sofa.

She sighed and stirred her beans. 'I can't stand the work at Arcis. I was hoping for something more challenging.'

'Well, tomorrow's another day.'

She looked up at him. 'I noticed you watching that

new girl, Anya.'

'I don't watch her.' At least he didn't think he did.

'It's a little creepy if you ask me.'

'What are you talking about?'

Sheila laughed. 'I've known you forever, Dom. I know you better than you know yourself.'

He huffed out a laugh and focused on the bread in his hand. 'Don't be stupid, Sheila. We're in Arcis for only one reason.'

'Still...'

'"Still" what?'

Sheila fluttered her eyelashes. 'I've seen that look before. You used to give it to me.'

'I never looked at you like that.'

'Okay, maybe not me. But you definitely looked at Kaylie that way.'

'I'm sorry, why are we even talking about this?'

Kaylie was beautiful like Sheila. She had long blonde hair and olive skin, and she was as tall as he was, with curves in all the right places. To this day, he still wondered why he hadn't noticed her before she became friends with Sheila. She was hard to miss.

Then there was short-haired Mia. She was quieter than Kaylie, who was more attention-seeking. Mia had been an interesting distraction for a while, but her shyness and inability to say what was on her mind frustrated the hell out of him. Kaylie, on the other hand, gossiped too much.

'Or maybe it's Mia you're thinking about?'

Sheila had never understood what he'd seen in quiet, shy Mia. Dom still didn't know what he'd seen in Kaylie.

She laughed. 'Ha! I can always get you to admit to it in the end.'

'I haven't admitted to anything, Sheila. And I don't need anyone drawing away my focus in Arcis.'

Dom shoved a spoonful of beans into his mouth.

'Then why are you blushing?' He looked away, causing Sheila to laugh. 'I was only kidding, Dominic. You know how I am. I like to get inside people's heads. It must be the mind manipulator in me.'

Sheila's parents, both psychologists, had been killed while hiking in the mountains more than two years earlier. A wild animal attack, the report had said. Dom's mother had taken her in soon after. When Mariella failed to return from Essention, Sheila and Dom had left Foxrush to seek help from the rumoured rebellion stronghold in the mountains. They returned unsuccessful only for the rebels —led by Max and Charlie—to arrive in their town soon after.

'Sometimes I think you enjoy making me squirm,' said Dom.

Sheila stood up and set her bowl down. 'It's always been our thing, Dominic.' She sashayed a little as she approached. Dom braced himself for what usually came next.

'Besides,' she said, kneeling in his lap, her legs either side of him. 'I don't like hearing about other girls. I prefer your focus only on me.'

He put the bowl on the floor and kept his hands flat on the sofa. She leaned over him, inching closer to his face. Her hair fell forward and she swept it back. She was stunning: pink lips, perfect bone structure, tall and lean with curves. Very similar to Kaylie.

'Sheila,' he said softly. 'That's enough.'

'Not until I say so.'

She moved her lips closer to his. Sheila liked to play this game often. But he was sick of her teasing.

He stared up at her in defiance. 'Go on. You're always threatening to do it. Kiss me.'

She flinched then regained her composure. 'I'm working up to it.'

He was done with these games. He gripped her hips and pulled her in closer.

'I want you, Sheila. I always have. Don't think I haven't noticed how you look now, how sexy you are.'

She smiled teasingly, keeping her focus on his neck.

'Look at me!' Her gaze trailed slowly from his neck up to his eyes. 'I want you. I need you to kiss me right now.'

She looked away and traced a finger along his cheek. 'Patience, Dominic. I'm working up to it.'

He kept hold of her and in one swift movement, he stood up. With one hand under her backside, he kept her legs wrapped around his waist.

Sheila stared at him. 'What are you doing?'

He didn't answer as he carried her to his bedroom, placed her on the bed and pushed her back until her head reached the pillow. Her eyes had widened and she was breathing hard. Sheila fought him a little, as she always did when they played, but Dom held her arms loosely above her head. He straddled her, his eyes never leaving hers.

She tried to shift away from him. 'Dom, I was only —'

'Teasing?'

'You know I was.'

'Sheila, we've been here a few times.' He looked around. 'Okay, maybe not in here exactly, but I can't stand it any longer. I need you to kiss me.'

'What?'

His nose grazed her cheek. 'Come on, don't tell me

you're not interested. Don't tell me this isn't what you want?'

Sheila's face softened into a smile. 'Of course it's what I want.'

She braved his gaze as he moved closer. His hands pinned her down lightly. Her chest rose and fell too fast.

Dom inched closer to her lips. The closer he got, the shorter Sheila's breaths became. He hovered above her, millimetres from her face.

She squeezed her eyes shut.

He moved to her neck, trailing kisses along her collarbone.

'Oh, God,' she said. 'Okay, I don't want this. Please.'

Dom shifted into a seated position and smiled at her. 'And why don't you want this?'

Sheila looked close to tears. 'I'm not going to say it.' He moved off her and lay beside her, his head on the pillow.

'Say it, for once.'

She shook her head, refusing to look at him. 'I don't want to.'

He propped himself up on one arm and turned her face, until she was looking at him. 'Why do you do that?'

'Do what?' Her eyes were strained, tearful.

'Pretend to be something you're not.'

She looked away. 'I'm not pretending.'

'Yes, you are. You pretend with me, but I know you too well. I can see it in your eyes. I can see you'd rather be somewhere else, with someone else.'

Her eyes were heavy with tears. 'Dom, please don't. I don't want to talk about it.'

'It's not my business, but don't lie to yourself. Please. Because it's who you are. I've always known it, even if you haven't.'

The tears fell and Sheila thumped him on the arm. 'Why did you go and make me cry?'

Dom smiled. 'It's what *I* do. Now, come here.' She turned and nestled into the crook of his arm. 'Do you know how creepy that was just now? You're like a sister to me.'

Sheila rocked with laughter. 'Yeah, it was pretty creepy.'

'Hey!'

Sheila sat up. 'Don't get me wrong, you're good-looking and all, but you're definitely not my type.'

'Not even with my girly hair?'

She tugged on one of his dreadlocks. 'Not even.'

'So, please, let's not do that again.'

Sheila lifted one eyebrow at him. 'Never say never. You know how I like my theatrics.'

Dom let out a sigh. 'Fine, but not like this. Now, out of my room, I want to get naked.'

Sheila dried her face with her hand and planted a kiss on his cheek. 'Sure thing, handsome.'

6

It wasn't the teenagers' fault they were in Arcis, and it wasn't their fault they were on Compliance. But Dom's clarity of mind made it hard for him to pretend to care about them, even though Max insisted he try. If interaction bettered his chances of rotation, he would fake it. Answers about his mother, about the whereabouts of Max's wife, existed on the ninth floor. Still on the ground floor, Dom hadn't even begun his journey yet.

The chatty murmurs of a few participants filled the atrium. Dom searched for another group to regale with his fake charm. He settled for a group of six; three boys were twirling their mops in a show for the three girls. Compliance appeared to enhance their stupidity while masking what they really were: pawns. He discreetly checked the position of the fixed camera up high. For the first time, he was pleased to see it track his movements.

He joined the back of their group as they chatted about the skills they'd learned in school before coming to Essention. It didn't surprise Dom to hear the girls had learned traditional skills like needlecraft, drawing and bookkeeping. The boys had learned bricklaying and carpentry.

Dom had shunned his father's advice and switched from a manual skill to music. And he'd received a set of bruises for his defiance. Since joining the rebels, he'd learned it was each man—or woman—for themselves. The tactical training helped him. So too did the physical workouts. If the shit hit the fan, he would be ready.

The girls noticed him first as he stood on the edge of the group. He smiled at one girl who smiled back and blushed. That seemed to anger the boys. Dom couldn't care less about the girls, or the fact that he'd undone the boys' efforts to impress with a simple smile. But three weeks had passed since the last rotation and he'd made no effort to talk to anyone except Sheila.

Anya didn't count; she was a loner like him. If the controllers in Arcis wanted to see interaction, he'd need to get in with a talkative group.

The group prattled on about their towns, what they used to do in school, their favourite teachers. This wasn't the first time he'd heard them mentioned the specifics. The participants were replaying the stories to each other, like they'd forgotten they'd discussed it last week, or the day before. Maybe Compliance messed with their memory too.

As he stood there, enduring the torture of stories with no substance, he wondered if there was another way to access the ninth floor. To bypass this charade and get the job done faster. His eyes grazed the hidden structure of Tower B. He'd seen the first-floor workers disappear inside it, but on the ground floor there was no similar access point.

The voices drifted away. Dom blinked and saw that the group had moved on, leaving him alone in the middle of the atrium. He blinked again and glanced up at the camera, hoping that was enough.

The Rebels

Ω

At lunch, Dom selected his food and looked around the dining hall for new people to annoy. Sheila's lunchtime companions were a bunch of girls who were hanging on her every word. She had a presence, and the girls wanted to be like her. Dom didn't know how she put up with the fake attention.

He spotted Anya sitting alone. As he walked past Sheila's table, she glanced up at him and gave him a wink. He slid into a seat opposite Anya. He wasn't sure when they'd started having lunch together; it had just happened. Something about her drew him in, and yet he knew nothing about her.

Anya eyed him cautiously, like she was trying to figure him out. His heart beat too hard whenever she got that look in her eye, like she was about to announce to the room, 'You're a rebel'. But she never did.

Anya nodded to Sheila. 'Why aren't you sitting with your friend over there?'

He pressed a hand to his heart. 'Because seeing you here all alone is doing terrible things to my conscience.'

Anya looked down. 'What has my being alone got to do with your conscience?'

Dom rubbed the back of his neck. 'Nothing. I was just being nice.'

Anya played with her food. 'I don't always like being alone. I know it looks like I do, but sometimes I need people.'

'Really?'

She glanced at him. 'Being alone makes me think too much about stuff. Bad things I couldn't control.'

'What things?'

Anya looked up and trapped him in her gaze. Those

eyes...

'Nothing.'

She dropped her gaze to her uneaten sandwich. He hated seeing her in pain.

'You know,' said Dom, 'I heard the wolves like to throw parties in that little alcove of theirs when we go home. Beer, chips, dip. It's a disgusting mess.'

Anya giggled. 'Yeah? A bit difficult to open beer, though, without opposable thumbs.'

It was Dom's turn to laugh. 'And when they want to have female wolves over, well, the space is a bit cramped. Tails get stuck in unmentionable places.'

Anya blushed. 'So they move the party into the atrium.' She clicked her fingers and her eyes widened. 'That's why the place is in such a mess when we get in each morning.'

Dom grinned at her. He liked this smiling version of her. He glanced over at Sheila and regretted it. She cocked an eyebrow at him, mouthing, *What the hell?* He ignored her and focused on Anya.

If she can have friends, so could he.

Dom leaned on the table. 'You keen to get to the next floor? I don't know about you, but I'm bored of the ground floor work.'

Anya shook her head and looked down. 'Not really. This is fine.'

He didn't believe her. 'You're happy pushing a mop around? I thought you were a girl with an adventurous spirit.'

She looked at him. The mask was back up. 'Yeah? And what do you know about me, Dom, other than the few things I've shared with you, which are pretty useless facts, by the way. I never hinted at an adventurous anything, so you must have made assumptions all on your own.'

'I'm not making assumptions.' His hands shook with anger. 'I see someone who is better than a cleaner for a bunch of robotic supervisors. I see someone who, given half the chance, would flip this place off and do something else.'

Anya frowned. 'That's where you're wrong, Dom. I'm not any of those things you say. I just wish everyone would leave me the hell alone.'

Her lips thinned and she stared at her lunch.

Dom wanted to yell at her. Break something. The table, maybe. *Jesus.* Why did this girl irritate him so much? So why the hell wasn't he walking away?

He sat there, just long enough to see her shoulders to relax. Then he got up and stormed out of the room.

Ω

Dom just wanted this day to be over. He opened the cleaning vestibule and pulled out a bucket and mop. Out of the corner of his eye, he caught Sheila on the move.

She slid in beside him. In a low whisper, she said, 'Hey, pretty boy, what's the deal with you and the short chick?'

'Her name's Anya.'

Sheila slid her gaze over to where Anya mopped her section. She had retreated into that shell of hers. He hated seeing how Compliance had dulled her energy.

God, he really wanted to make her angry, to make her feel something.

Sheila cut through his thoughts. 'She doesn't look like your usual type.'

'What's my usual type?'

Sheila shrugged. 'Tall, curvy, long hair. Like Kaylie. Like me. Not short-haired Mia. She was too quiet for you.' She glanced over again. 'That one looks like she has a rod up her butt.'

'You don't know her.'

Her hazel gaze pinned him to the wall. 'I don't like how you lose focus around her. She's getting under your skin. Be careful or you might let something slip about our extracurricular activities.'

'I hadn't planned on it, Sheila,' he hissed. 'I'm doing the same as you, making friends. Get off my back.'

She scoffed, drawing eyes to their discussion. 'You're getting pretty pally with each other. Watch what you say to her.'

'I've got this. *Jesus.* Put a little faith in me.'

Sheila softened her stance. She had every right to be angry. Any slip up on his part would affect her too.

'Okay. Because it's you. But I'm keeping an eye on you. If I hear you getting too chatty, I'm telling Max and Charlie.'

Dom cupped her face. It was the only way to calm her down when she was livid. The other girls turned to watch, shooting eye daggers at Sheila.

Except for Anya, who wasn't looking at all.

Ω

Dom and Sheila stood together on the Monorail platform after their shift and waited for the train. Anya stood a few feet away, but didn't notice them.

On board the train, the air felt tight. He pulled out the band securing his dreadlocks and shook out his hair. For the first time, he considered chopping them off. The participants were packed into the carriage like beans in a can, leaving them little space to move or talk privately. Dom inched closer to the door where there was a little space. Sheila followed and they leaned into each other, pretending to be more than friends.

'I'm worried about Anya,' said Dom in her ear.

Sheila pulled back from him. 'You like her! And you're going to blow our cover.'

'No, I don't. She just reminds me of how I felt before you showed up in Arcis. I don't want her to get left behind. Maybe if we talk a little, Arcis will see and rotate her.'

'So what if she is alone? So what if she gets left behind? Why is it your business?'

Anya's attitude at lunch bothered him. Compliance made the participants too accepting of their situation. But Anya was different: angry, sad. It worried him that her reasons for staying had nothing to do with the drug.

'She doesn't want to leave. She's preparing to stay on the ground floor forever.'

'Why is that a bad thing, Dom? Don't get me wrong, I'm as curious as the next person, but what's happening on the floors above scares the crap out of me.'

'Me, too. But I don't see how this programme ends without going through all nine floors. We may have entered the place to do a job, but I can't stand to see anyone left behind.'

Sheila snorted; several boys looked her way. She smiled sweetly at them until they blushed and looked elsewhere. 'Is it that you can't stand to see anyone left behind, or you can't stand to see *her* left behind? Admit it, Dom. You have a thing for Miss Prim and Proper.'

Dom rolled his eyes. 'I don't. But I do need a favour from you. It'll require you putting that scheming brain of yours to work.'

Sheila leaned in closer. 'I'm listening.'

'I need to do something to get her to care. I can't

progress knowing she might be the only innocent person left behind.'

Sheila snorted. 'Innocent, my ass.'

'Please, Sheila. I need your help.'

She bit her lip. 'I'm not happy you're losing focus over a girl, but, anything to get you back on track. As long as that's all it is: losing focus.'

When Anya made it to the first floor in Arcis, she would be on her own. He and Sheila had a job to do and it didn't involve babysitting her.

'Thanks. It is, I swear.'

Sheila smirked and stepped closer to him. 'Don't thank me yet. You might not like what I have planned. In my experience, there's only one thing guaranteed to work with hormonal girls on Compliance.'

She cupped the back of his neck and pressed her body to his.

'How do you feel about a lot of flirting and touching while we're at Arcis?'

7

Dom arrived an hour early for his shift the next day. The place was quiet and it was rare to have the changing room all to himself. He undressed and slipped on the overalls that ended up more wet than dirty at the end of a shift. Most of the rooms in this place were off limits, except for the changing room and the dining hall in the atrium. He used the quiet time to check the walls, looking for a way out or up.

The door opened suddenly and a rotund man with thinning brown hair and red cheeks entered. He wore an all-black tunic with gold buttons and trim. He looked vaguely familiar.

'Can I help you?' Dom said, fixing his pose.

'Dom Pavesi, come with me.'

The man turned and left.

Dom's heart kicked up a gear as he fixed the strap on his overalls into place. He stepped outside into the lobby to see the man was standing by the elevator. It was open and he gestured for him to enter.

He slowed his approach, not sure why he was being singled out for attention.

The man rolled his hand at him. 'Hurry, please.'

Dom entered it along with the man and the doors closed. A second later, the doors opened out into a changing room.

The man exited with a command to follow. Dom hurried to keep up. He led him through a door to the right and into what looked like an office.

Inside the space were a table and two chairs. The man gestured for Dom to sit. He did, reluctantly while the uniformed male perched on the edge of the table, hands clasped on his lap.

'My name is Supervisor One. The controllers of Arcis asked me to talk to you.'

His heart pounded loudly in his ears. 'Yeah?'

'They wanted me to ask you some questions.'

He swallowed. 'About what?'

The supervisor rolled his eyes, as if the reason was ridiculous. 'About your hair of all things.'

'My hair? What about it?'

'They notice you keep it long while the others have theirs short. Why?'

He knew the real reason, but no way he would tell anyone why. 'I like to try new things.'

The man leaned in. 'Is it because of your father?'

Dom jerked back from him. A breath rushed out of his mouth. 'Excuse me?'

'The controllers in Arcis like to know where the participants come from. Mariella and Carlo were your parents, no?'

'Yes,' he answered slowly.

'Please don't worry, Dominic. The controllers of Arcis like to know who comes into not only their urbano but their training programme.'

He lost the ability to speak. Was this the end? Would they kill him now, or make him disappear like they had Mariella?

His nostrils flared. 'Have I done something wrong?'

The supervisor laughed suddenly. 'No. The controllers are curious about you, about why you don't blend in.' He waved a hand around the room. 'As you can see, this place isn't big on personality. The controllers want to understand why you resist.'

'I... didn't know I was resisting. I'm doing the work.' He played up his ignorance. 'Is there a problem with my work? Is that what this is about?'

The supervisor shook his head. 'Far from it. You're the hardest worker on the floor. But'—he leaned in closer—'if you want to progress, I'd think about changing your attitude.'

He leaned back, allowing Dom a chance to take a breath.

'Point taken. Can I go now?'

The man touched his ear, as though someone spoke to him. 'Yes. The others will be arriving soon. Take the lift back down. Be ready to get to work. Rotation is coming soon.'

The man stood up and gestured to the door. Dom got to his feet and offered a quick smile before he left through it.

In the lift, he touched his snarled hair. Carlo might be dead but he was still making life difficult for him.

Ω

Rotation arrived two days later and Dom and Sheila made it to the first floor. He'd been delaying the decision all week, but he couldn't go through another interrogation with the supervisor. He hadn't told Sheila what the man had said. He didn't want to worry her.

Anya hadn't been successful in rotating, but with eyes on him Dom had to focus on blending in.

Each step to Charlie and Max's place filled him with dread. It had taken him a year to grow his hair out.

Eleven steps from the front garden to the back door.

Charlie waited for him in the kitchen. Dom flashed him a quick smile.

'You look like you're about to be sick.' He pulled a chair over and guided Dom into it.

'I might be if I think about it for too long.'

'Any reason for the change of heart?'

'No, I just realised I needed to conform a little more.' He'd barely slept as he replayed the conversation between him and the supervisor, who he later remembered from the hospital. He and a woman had injected the orphans with their chips.

Charlie placed his wrinkled hands on Dom's shoulders. 'Don't worry I'm good at what I do. I've cut many styles over my time as a barber. Trust me, many of them were a lot more complicated than what you want me to do.'

His hands on him were meant to reassure, but the weight only added to his worry.

Dom took a deep breath. 'I know. I just don't want to regret this decision.'

Charlie opened a drawer and took out a pair of scissors. Beads of sweat rolled down Dom's back. The overhead light glinted off the metal.

Why was he even doing this? What did he care what the controllers thought of him?

'You have to go deeper,' said Charlie, as if he'd heard his silent question. 'You need to blend in more.'

That was why.

'I know.'

'You could have done this yourself.'

'No, I couldn't.'

'Are you sure about this?'

Dom closed his eyes and nodded. 'You're the only one I trust to do it right.'

Charlie separated one of the dreadlocks and snipped it off at the base. Dom opened his eyes as Charlie handed it to him. With his hair short, he knew he looked just like Carlo. The sick feeling returned and he closed his eyes again. But as Charlie continued, Dom's head began to feel lighter, in more ways than one.

The old man handed Dom a mirror and he winced. Carlo was there, all right, but he could also see the features he'd inherited from his mother. Charlie had snipped the hair off roughly; a bit of work was still needed to fix the style.

A rattling noise startled the pair. Both men snapped their gazes to the back door.

'Stay here,' said Charlie. Still holding the scissors in his hand, he jerked the door open.

Dom dashed to the living room and eased back the curtain. A terrified-looking Anya ran out of the gate and blended into the shadows. He smiled and shook his head. Had his and Sheila's plan to flirt really worked? Did she care about moving on now?

A new fire ignited within him at the prospect of finding out.

He returned to the kitchen, running through what he and Charlie had discussed and what Anya might have overheard. Despite Sheila's warnings to him about revealing to anyone who they were, Dom ached to connect with someone on a deeper level. Anya had her own secrets. Could he trust her with his?

'It was just an animal,' he said as Charlie closed the

back door. 'I saw it scurrying out the gate.'

'That's probably what it was.' Charlie gestured for him to sit back down. 'Now sit. We're not done.'

Charlie swapped the scissors for a hair trimmer. 'I'll have to buzz-cut this. When your hair's grown out again, I'll give you a proper style.' He started the trimmer and ran it over Dom's head. 'Why did you grow it out in the first place?'

'My father hated long hair on boys and I couldn't think of a better way to remember him.'

Yes, Carlo had hated it. After a year-long drinking binge, Carlo had emerged from his haze and noticed a six-year-old Dom with hair so long it fell into his eyes. Dom had wanted to grow it out and Mariella was letting him. Then one night, Carlo, still drunk from the day before, had dragged him out of bed and sat him in a chair. He told him he looked like a girl, then took a pair of garden shears and cut off every last bit of hair, removing some skin in the process. That night, Dom cried in the arms of his mother. He hadn't known what hurt worse: being called a girl by the father he looked up to, or the weeping cuts left behind from Carlo's clumsy technique.

'You don't talk about him much,' said Charlie.

'Talking would give that man the time of day and he doesn't deserve it.' Charlie knew the basics: that Carlo had been an alcoholic and hit Dom and his mother on occasion. Dom had also told him and Max about his surgeries, when Max noticed his scars.

'You can't hold on to the past, son. It will eat you alive.'

'I've done okay, so far.'

Charlie paused his cutting and leaned against the counter facing him. 'Doing okay and living to your full potential are two different things. What that man did to you was unforgivable, but he's dead now. He's responsible for it all: the surgeries, the suffering he caused her. Even so, you need to move on with your life.'

Dom shook his head. 'I can't. Not while my mother is still missing.'

Charlie's pale blue eyes hid sadness. He had a way of saying so little yet so much. He was the opposite of his asshole father who could never shut up.

'What happened to him?'

'He died.' *Because I killed him.*

'How? You said he was reported missing, and then he turned up dead in the middle of the woods?'

Dom lifted both brows at Charlie. 'Why do you need to know what happened to him? Isn't it enough he's gone?'

'I suppose so, but you should be happier he's out of your life. But he still has a hold over you. I'm wondering why.'

Because of what I did, Charlie. I lured the bastard who tormented me and my mother out to that place and I ended his life.

'He's been inside my head for so long, I guess it'll take some time to get him out of there.'

Charlie nodded and placed a heavy hand on his shoulder. 'What you suffered... I can't imagine putting Max through that. You're a strong man, Dominic.'

Dom swallowed back the bile that rose every time he thought about Carlo. He needed to forget about him.

Charlie finished cutting Dom's hair and got out the sweeping brush.

Dom stood and moved the chair out of the way. 'Why did you become a barber?'

Charlie chuckled. 'It was to meet a girl, actually.'

'Really?'

'She was the daughter of the barbershop owner in Greenacre, where I grew up. I wanted to ask her out, but I couldn't figure out how to do it. So I applied for a job there.'

'So she was Max's mother?'

Charlie barked out a laugh. 'Heck, no! I was in lust. She spent most of her time working as a teacher in a bunch of other towns. I thought it was a noble profession until she came home one weekend with her fiancé. My jaw nearly hit the floor.'

'So you quit?'

He nodded. 'I moved to Halforth. Turns out they all had really bad hair there. I set up my own barbershop and the rest is history.'

Dom laughed hard at the image of a town of people with untamed locks. 'Bad hair?'

'Shockingly so. Lucky I got there when I did. Those folks hadn't seen a stylist in forever. I learned how to cut women's hair, too. Really enjoyed it. They would come in every week, tell me about their days. I loved the interaction more than the hair cutting, if that's even possible.'

Dom shuddered at the idea of listening to everyone else's problems. In some way, he was grateful the participants were on Compliance. Problems didn't exist on Compliance. Yet, Anya seemed to be sabotaging her own progress in Arcis well enough.

He wanted to know why.

'We brought in a new girl from the camp,' said Charlie. 'She joined Arcis when you and Sheila rotated.'

Dom's heart thumped. Please not Kaylie or Mia. Whatever they had was in the past.

'Who?'

'June Shaw.'

Dom breathed a sigh of relief. He liked June. Even better, Sheila liked June. She would fit in perfectly. Her pale blonde hair and blue eyes gave her the right amount of innocence. But June was far from innocent. She was competitive, and Dom had raced to assemble guns faster than her in the rebel camp. June had won every time. Apparently, her uncle had taught her how to disassemble a firearm as soon as she was old enough.

'June is a good fit. She'll make friends easy.'

'She'll be doing more than making friends. I've asked her to get close to specific people, in particular a girl called Tahlia Odare, who started at the same time. Her parents lived in Praesidium for a short while before being sent back to their town.'

Dom hadn't heard of any families living in the city being sent back. 'Why?'

'That's what we want to know. If you're in the capital city, it's usually to stay. Something must have happened.'

Charlie checked his watch and ushered Dom to the door. 'Best you get going, now. The scanners are due to carry out their sweep in half an hour. I want you back in East when they locate you.'

8

Sheila blocked Dom's access to the food counter. 'Are you freaking serious?' She was glaring at him, her arms folded.

He pushed past her to grab lunch for the two of them. The first-floor dining hall was packed with boys wearing ill-fitting suits and girls in blouse/skirt combinations. They'd been on the floor for a week now.

He loosened the tie around his neck that cut off his blood supply. 'Let's go outside to talk. Too many people here.'

The first floor was a strange place. Their job was to race between a terminal room and a storage room to collect a folder with the right barcode on the front. The purpose was to scan the barcode before the terminal clock ran out. Easy.

They rode the elevator down to the lobby. Sheila followed him outside and Dom found a secluded section of grass. He set down both their lunches. Sheila dropped to the ground with a huff. He handed her a sandwich and a bottle of water and she grimaced. With the antidote to Compliance in their systems, the food tasted strange. Sweeter. But it was either this or starvation.

'I'm not sure I heard you correctly, Dominic.'

'Yeah, you did.'

'You're not seriously going to do it?'

'Why not? She could be useful.'

Sheila snorted. 'Little Miss Goody Two-Shoes is about as useful as a nun in a brothel.' She shook her head. 'I forbid it. It's not just your ass you're putting on the line. What if she tells Arcis about us?'

'She won't.'

'How the hell do you know? You've only known her for a month.'

'I have a good feeling about her.'

It had been a week since Anya had followed him to Charlie and Max's house. The fact that she had meant Compliance wasn't affecting her like the others. It also hinted that there could be more to this girl. He'd pitched a new plan to Sheila that went beyond their flirting. Or rather, Sheila had been flirting and Dom went along with it. She enjoyed her dramatics too much.

She stared down at her sandwich, still in its wrapper. 'I'll continue to play your little game to move her on, but she's on her own. I forbid you to tell her what we are.'

What was he supposed to do? He and Sheila needed to venture deeper into the operations at Arcis. Why couldn't she see his plan was the best option, and that they could do with all the allies they could get? But telling Anya could also backfire.

Dom leaned back on his hands and sighed. He hated it when Sheila was right.

She eyed him. 'It's that new haircut of yours, which I think is *très* sexy, by the way. But it's making you act like a dingbat all of a sudden.'

Dom ran his hand over his hair. 'You like the new cut?' He'd almost tried to tie it back that morning.

She fanned her face. 'Of course, darling. It does special things to me. Now, stop trying to change the subject. What are you *not* going to do?'

'I won't tell her.'

'Good. Speaking of which, here comes the nun now.'

Dom's heart thumped a little faster when Anya rounded the corner. She had her lunch under one arm, her posture hunched as though she carried more than food. She glanced at a group of boys playing cards. Then her eyes found him, Sheila next. She straightened up and looked away.

'You owe me big for this one, you idiot,' said Sheila as she stood up.

'Hey, skinny girl! It's Anya, right?'

Anya stopped in her tracks, her unease clear. Dom hated the pretence, and the way Sheila pushed her buttons. Anya was quiet, unwilling to fight, or do anything. So why was he letting Sheila do this?

Because he sensed that beneath the quiet exterior was something else, and he needed proof it existed.

Anya stopped and gave Sheila her best fake smile. 'Sheila. *So* nice to see you again.'

There's my girl.

Jesus! Focus, Pavesi.

'Sorry you can't sit with Dom anymore,' said Sheila. 'You obviously weren't good enough to make it to the first floor.'

He stopped short of giving Sheila a withering look or a punch to the arm. She was being a bitch.

Stop complaining, Dom. You asked her to do this.

He stared down at his hands.

Sheila laughed once. 'You know you only got into this programme because your parents are dead.'

Okay, that's taking it too far.

'Sheila, that's enough,' said Dom softly. He didn't want Sheila to stop, just to pull it back a little.

She ignored him, squaring up to Anya. 'Your parents were killed and you're here because they had nowhere else to put the ugly kids.'

Anya's face changed from pale to a deep shade of red. She ground two fists into the sides of her legs.

A non-Compliance reaction. Interesting.

'There's a reason you're still on the ground floor. It's because you're not good enough to do *anything*. Okay, so you can push a mop around a floor, but that's it. They feel sorry for you because you're such a loser.'

Jesus, Sheila. Rein it in.

He opened his mouth to say something but stopped. Anything he said now would ruin this moment.

Anya snorted with laughter. Dom snapped his attention back to her.

'What's so funny, loser?' said Sheila.

'Nothing, I was just picturing you taking your pet for a walk, that's all.' Anya glanced at Dom. He stared at her, absorbing this new angry version of her—a girl with a ballsy attitude and an ability to surprise him. He leaned back on his arms, trying to hide the smile that tugged at his mouth.

Sheila poked her finger hard into Anya's chest. Anya stepped out of her space. But she wasn't backing away from Sheila—she was making the space her own.

'You can't talk to me like that, *loser*,' said Sheila. 'You're just jealous that Dom doesn't want to hang around with you anymore. And that's all it is. *Hanging around*. He would never want to be with someone as childish as you.'

A look of hurt flashed across Anya's face. It was so

fleeting, he almost didn't catch it. He was about to tell Sheila off a second time when she jabbed at Anya again. Something in her brain switched, turning her from a compliant worker into a normal human being. When Anya grabbed Sheila's finger and twisted her arm behind her back, his eyes widened.

'Get off me!' said Sheila. She wasn't playing anymore.

Anya, who was shorter than Sheila, held her off with one arm.

Damn, that girl is strong. He pulled back his excitement.

Anya caught the back of Sheila's knees and eased her down onto the ground. As Anya straightened up, she was shaking. Her face was flushed and she was breathing heavily. She flashed him a cynical look, to which he responded with a smile.

Screw Sheila. Screw the plan. He wanted to tell her everything, about Mariella, about the rebellion. He wanted to spill about what Max and Charlie believed Praesidium was doing. Mariella would have liked Anya.

His heart ached. He was thinking about his mother as if she was already dead.

Anya stormed off and Dom tried to help Sheila to her feet. She waved off his assistance with a huff.

'I think I hate that girl even more than I did before. Did you see what she did to me?' She rubbed her shoulder. 'She almost broke my arm.'

'I think you're exaggerating a little.'

Sheila's look was venomous. 'You are not telling that little witch anything. You hear me?'

Yeah, he heard her.

Sheila leaned into him for support as they walked back inside—part of the dramatics. 'Now, come on. Let's play this up for the cameras. I get the feeling this place likes the drama we teenagers create.'

They made it inside. He jerked back when he saw Anya standing just inside the door. He kept his gaze low as he passed, but caught the look Sheila gave Anya.

What was she feeling now? Regret? Anger? Nothing at all? With one look he could check. They slipped inside the elevator and rode it to the first floor.

'You want that psycho on the first floor? Are you crazy, Dom?'

'Sheila, I love you, but you can be judgemental at times. You went a bit overboard back there.'

She shook out her hands. 'Call it me getting into character.'

'Then, you can't be surprised if things spiral out of control.'

The elevator door opened and they crossed the changing room floor.

'How about I don't say anything to her about things and you give her a chance?' said Dom.

Sheila mulled it over. 'Okay. But I'm telling you right now. That girl isn't worth your time.'

9

The guilt was eating him up.

He'd made a promise to Sheila. And he'd broken that promise last night.

Anya had followed him to Charlie's again. Maybe her confrontation with Sheila had woken up something inside her, maybe it hadn't. But it had stirred a need inside him, so deep that he'd headed to the factory instead of going back to the apartment. There, Dom had donned a pair of boxing gloves and hit the bag a few times. Then Anya had shown up. It had played out exactly as he'd hoped.

It frustrated him that he couldn't read her as easily as he could the other girls. Even Kaylie and Mia had been open books, despite their efforts not to be. He'd told Anya too much about himself. He'd mentioned setting up her fight with Sheila to get her to care more. He'd almost let slip about his and Sheila's true intentions.

But while she was still on Compliance, he had to be careful around her. The brain processed things differently while on the drug; it gave her a hazy perspective and muddled up what the real threats were.

He stood next to Sheila in the terminal room on the

first floor while they waited for the last person to make it back and scan their file.

She elbowed him. 'What's up with you? You're acting weird today.'

He frowned at her. 'Nothing. What's up with you?'

'I'm all good.'

Brianna burst through the doors, the youngest on this floor at sixteen. Her long, brown hair billowed behind her. Her eyes were too wide. She slammed into the terminal and groped for the scanner. She pressed it while he and fifteen others looked on. The clock counted down the last thirty seconds.

Dom hated this. He looked away. But Sheila looked on, looking ready to help the girl.

But she didn't. None of them ever helped.

The timed work hadn't changed since he started over a week ago and Dom could find no relevance to it. All he knew was the participants had to beat the clock. If the clock ran out, the terminal would shock them. The countdown time changed at will and almost all of them had received a shock, except for Dom and Sheila. Not being on Compliance gave them a secret advantage.

He assumed Arcis had picked him for rotation because he'd made friends.

Or he could have been just a random pick.

The clock started over after Brianna dropped her file in the box on the side of the table. Everyone geared up to run again. Brianna's chest heaved, as though she could use a minute. But the clock restarted at six minutes—the same as before

Sheila sprinted out the door; Dom followed her. As he ran, he wondered about the floors above. Would they all be timed runs like this? The ground floor had been the exception.

So far, the days between rotation had been consistent: between twenty-five and thirty days. He'd reported that detail back to Max. Rebels were stationed in one of the towns beyond Essention. Max had instructed them to work out how Arcis operated.

Dom burst into the records room and slipped into hunt mode. Sheila was already up on one of the ladders searching for her file. Sheila had struggled with the idea of shocks more than Dom. He knew they reminded her of a bad time in her life, in her early teens when she'd started to notice girls for the first time. Her parents had signed her up for shock therapy to "cure" her of her affliction. She'd begged them to stop. She even got a boyfriend so they would believe the cure had worked. But they'd continued with the treatment that turned her from a ballsy girl into a meek, withdrawn one.

Dom found his file and ran back to the terminal room. He and Sheila scanned their barcodes and dropped the files into the box at the side of the terminal. Brianna burst through the door with her file last, looking ready to collapse.

The lunchtime bell rang and with it the clock stopped. An exhausted Dom followed Sheila to the dining hall. On the ground floor they had pretended to be a couple, but without Anya to see it, Dom had lost the motivation to keep up the pretence. He'd done all he could to shock her into action. And it had worked.

For the most part.

'I'm so sick of this floor,' said Sheila. 'I don't mind a bit of manual labour, but I'm freaking out about that clock, like it's gonna catch me out. Have you seen how pale Brianna looks?'

'I know, but concentrate. It might happen, it might not.'

'Easy for you to say. Nothing scares you, except...' Her eyes raked over his T-shirt, which hid the scar on his stomach and he shivered. 'The chance of that happening in here is probably quite low.'

The thought had crossed his mind, but he'd pushed it away. Yet, with a single look, Sheila had undone those efforts.

'I'm living my worst nightmare on this floor,' said Sheila, pouting. 'And you don't even care.'

'Of course I care. But we can't do anything about it. We can't influence the outcome. If Arcis wants to shock us, it will.'

'Says Mister Control over here. You're telling me you're fine playing those odds?'

No, but he'd gone over every detail in his head looking for a way to cheat the system. He'd come up with nothing.

Sheila played with her food. She propped up her head with her hand and sighed. Dom considered going outside to look for Anya. He'd taken a girl he hardly knew to the secret running track and playground. He hadn't told Max, but he suspected Charlie knew when he dropped the key back after. All he'd asked him was how the running had gone. But it was the way he asked.

Charlie was the father he should have had.

Sheila sighed loudly and pushed her food away. Her irritable mood on this floor got on his last nerve.

'Eat something.' He shoved her food back to her. 'You're more likely to slip up if you're tired *and* hungry.'

She shot him a poisonous look, but it didn't last. Her moods with him never did, because he refused to take her bullshit. With others, it was easier for her to let the bad fester. Sheila was worse than a child at times. Demanding. He'd confronted her many times in their teens whenever she acted like a brat. But he hadn't known what her parents had put her through. She'd stayed silent on all of it until one day, when she was fourteen, she'd blurted it out to him.

'They don't understand me,' she had said, sobbing. '*I* don't even freaking understand me. I'm trying to be what they want me to be, but it's hard. They keep taking me to a specialist. I don't like him. After the treatment he tries to get me alone. Touches my knee. Says there are other ways to cure me.'

Dom had asked for the doctor's name. Gone to his house. Stood outside the window. Watched him eat dinner with his wife and kids. Followed him for a week. Took some compromising photos of him and another woman. Left threatening notes in his letterbox. Told him if he didn't back off, he would kill him. It had worked for a week, until the doctor resumed his normal duties, including seeing Sheila as a patient. Her parents had stopped going to the clinic on the doctor's orders, so Dom accompanied her to her next appointment. The doctor had ordered him to be removed from the clinic, but Dom showed him a few snaps of him and the other woman. It was enough to get Sheila reassigned to another doctor.

Two years later, her parents died while exploring in a nearby mountain range with a hiking group. The easiest thing to do would have been to bring Sheila home. But he couldn't subject her to the abuse of his father. So Sheila lived at home for the next six months while Dom brought her food. That's when Mariella found out and took her in. Carlo had gone on one of his regular drinking benders and never knew anything about it.

Now, inside a place with no obvious motive, Sheila's refusal to eat pissed him off. 'Sheila! Eat something now. Or I'll—'

She looked up at him. 'Or you'll what?'

'I'll take you over my knee and spank you.'

She stared at him then burst into laughter. 'God, Dom, you used to be so much better at dishing out threats. What happened to you?'

Dom grinned. 'You've heard them all. I needed to try a new one.'

Sheila bit into her sandwich. 'Well, it worked. If you can believe that.'

They ate their lunch in silence. Dom's control slipped to think of Anya. What was she doing right now? Was she thinking about the self-defence lessons he'd given her last night? They'd ended up in the abandoned playground. Alone. Her body, pressed up against his, did dangerous things to him, things that risked distracting him from his true purpose. She must have felt his reaction to her in more ways than one.

Of course she had, Pavesi. She wriggled like a wild cat. She couldn't put enough distance between you.

He'd even grabbed her hand. He hadn't planned it, it just happened, but she'd pulled her hand out of his.

God, why did she make him feel like a perverted schoolboy?

Because you are, Pavesi. You're the worst kind. You can't get this girl out of your head and she's sending you signals to stay away. Yet you keep going back for more punishment because, Christ, it wouldn't be you if you didn't put yourself through this crap at least once a week. If it's not her, it's remembering what you did to your father.

His feelings for Anya and what happened to Carlo were not the same. One was about new beginnings; the other was about burying the past.

When he'd asked Charlie for a spare dosage of the

antidote, Charlie had hesitated. So, while Anya had waited for him to drop the key back, he'd stolen one from Charlie's special hiding spot, in the floor space hidden beneath the living room carpet. The old man would notice the missing vial, but Dom hoped to use it before he could do anything about it.

He excused himself from the table and told Sheila he'd see her back inside. Needing a quiet moment, he took the lift downstairs. A part of him was hoping to see Anya again, but a part of him hoped she wasn't there. He didn't want to be wrong about her.

The lift opened and Dom heard voices. Two.

He recognised one as Ash, the boy from the ground floor. He and a second boy were chatting outside. Both had their backs turned to the door.

While they were distracted, Dom slipped inside the changing room. They entered the lobby and stopped outside the changing room door.

'It's not like that,' said Ash to the boy with strawberry-blond hair. He'd seen him in Anya's group. Warren something.

'Then what is it like? This place is a joke.'

Ash shushed him. 'It's a game, Warren. That's all. Play it their way and you'll be home free. Make friends, show them you're interested in the people here.'

Warren snorted. 'It's a bit hard when the people you've been stuck with don't include you in anything.'

'Find someone who will get you rotated faster.'

'Like who?'

It was Ash's turn to snort. 'The loner in the group always works well for me.'

Dom clenched his fists. While Ash hadn't mentioned anyone by name, Anya was the most obvious choice for Warren to target. It worried him that he knew nothing about him.

All the more reason to give Anya the antidote. He just needed to find the right time.

Warren said, 'I suppose there is someone... And you're sure that she'll guarantee rotation?'

Ash laughed lightly. 'Not exactly, but she will help. The people in here are a means to an end. Everyone has a purpose. Remember that.'

Dom heard new movement and stepped back into the room. His heart pounded as he waited for Warren to find him in a changing room he had no business being in. But nobody came in. Instead, he heard the lift moving. Dom peeked out to find the lobby empty. He called the lift and waited.

Halfway across the first-floor walkway, the bell sounded. He glanced down to see the ground floor participants had gathered. His gaze found Anya's group. She had her back to the walkway. Warren was standing next to her, chatting and elbowing her.

Dom walked on, clenching and unclenching his fists.

He arrived back in the terminal room to find a frowning Sheila waiting.

'Cutting it fine, weren't you?'

'I just needed some fresh air.'

Brianna waited by her terminal, too pale, too skinny and with a wild fearful look in her eye. She was just a kid. They all were. Dom wished he could shield her from the misery of this place. But he had a job to do and it didn't include fixing the problems of others. He and Sheila must push on to reach the ninth floor.

The people in here are a means to an end. Everyone has a purpose.

Dom hated to admit it but Ash might be right.

The terminals started up and Sheila perked up. She stared at the screen, then glanced at Dom to give him a nod. He nodded back, once. Nothing more. With two cameras—one visible, one hidden—watching over the room, he wasn't sure what Arcis hoped to see.

Five minutes flashed up on-screen. One minute less than before lunch. Arcis appeared to drop the timer when someone hadn't been shocked for a few days. Brianna was the last to have received a shock. It was almost as if Arcis wanted another incident to happen.

Brianna tensed up and tugged on the ends of her long hair. She looked around, looked back at the screen. Her eyes were stuck on wide. A file number flashed up below the timer, which started the countdown. Sheila bolted out of the room and Dom grabbed Brianna's hand.

'Come on, let's do this one together.'

The girl looked up at him like he was some kind of hero. He was anything but. Brianna's hand was cold and thin in his. She kept up with him, fuelled on by having someone at her side. They made it to the records room and Dom found Brianna's file first. He handed it to her then told her to run. Her lips pulled up into a faint smile as she disappeared through the doors back to the terminal room.

He counted across the rows for his own file and found it quickly enough. Sheila was beside him with hers. They ran back to the room and scanned their files with thirty seconds left on the clock. The others made it back and stopped their clocks. But Dom's clock kept counting down. He picked up the scanner again and pressed the button. The red crosshatch lit up the barcode on the front of the file. It even registered his attempt with a beep. But still his clock counted backwards. Five, four, three...

A deep whir came from inside his terminal. Sparks jumped from it to his hand, snapping him into place. He gritted his teeth against the electricity that made his hand throb. The surge snapped at him, shaking his bones. All he could move were his eyes. He looked at the scanner in his hand and willed himself to drop it.

But nothing worked. Not his arms, not his legs. He yelled out a scream through clenched teeth. Hot electricity pulsed through his body, searching for a way out. Flashes of red caught his eye as the time counter flash repeatedly at zero. The flesh where his hand gripped the scanner burned. Air caught in his lungs, tightened his chest and made it hard to breathe. The electricity continued to hold him up like he was some kind of doll.

It released its hold suddenly and the invisible strings snapped. He crumpled in a heap. Sheila lunged for him and protected his head before it hit the floor. He heard new voices. Strange people in white boiler suits hovered over him.

Dom closed his eyes and the voices drifted away.

10

Dom woke up in a bed with a closed curtain around it. Other people were close by; he could hear them moving. He inspected the damage on his hand, but found only unblemished skin. No pain either.

Dom got up and yanked back the curtain.

'Wait now,' said a boy with blond hair wearing a white boiler suit. 'You're not supposed to be up.'

'Where am I? What am I doing here?'

'Protocol. You're supposed to stay here after an electric shock. They need to monitor you.'

Dom blinked. 'But I feel fine. Why do I feel fine? I should be...'

Dead? Injured? Suffering from horrible burns at least.

'It's Praesidium's medicine. Heals everything. The team gave you a shot to counteract the effects of an electric shock. It steadies any heart arrhythmia you might have. The paste takes care of any wounds.'

Dom stared at his hand again, the one that had melded with the scanner. It looked like nothing had happened.

He stepped forward, prompting the boy to block

him. 'You can't leave the infirmary. Not until they say so.'

'Who says I can't?'

Dom pushed past him to the door, but at the exit he hesitated. He was supposed to be on Compliance. That meant living up to the drug's name.

Screw it, I need to see Sheila.

A female supervisor appeared at the door and interrupted his plans for escape. She wore a similar black tunic—gold trim and buttons—to the man who'd cornered him over a week ago. 'Is there a problem in here?'

The boy dropped his gaze to the ground. 'No, ma'am. I was just explaining to the patient—'

'I'll take over. You go on now.'

The boy hurried away.

Dom stood face-to-face with the supervisor. She was new.

'You are Dominic Pavesi, correct?' Her cold blue eyes unsettled him.

'Yes. Where am I?'

'You're in the infirmary on the second floor. You must return to your bed.'

'But I feel fine.'

The supervisor placed a hand on his shoulder. It turned to ice beneath her touch. 'Quick recovery and relapse are two related things. I must insist you stay here until you are well enough to return to your duties. The health of the participants is our top priority.'

'Is that why you shock them?'

The supervisor's gaze hardened and Dom froze.

Careful, Pavesi.

'The shocks are not meant to harm, but to remind the participant that tardiness is not permitted on the first floor. If you are asked to complete a timed task and you fail in that completion, there will be consequences. It is no different from what would happen in the real world.'

'Is it what happens in Praesidium?'

The supervisor's thin mouth pulled up into a strange smile. Dom shivered.

'Praesidium runs as efficiently as it can with humans living there. The Collective that runs Praesidium has learned to expect less from humans. It is rarely disappointed. Arcis is designed to be efficient. We are trying to push you out of your comfort zone so you will find your path, your true purpose in life.'

The Collective? Dom returned to his bed. With the supervisor following him, he didn't have much choice.

'Teenagers are known to mess up,' said Dom. 'Has your *Collective* taken that into account?'

'Of course. Nothing happens here that participants won't be able to handle.'

Dom's heart thumped harder. 'But it wasn't always teenagers. I mean, I heard there used to be adults in here.'

The supervisor appeared to think about it. 'Once, perhaps. The towns are no longer safe because of the rebel activity. Arcis has adapted to fit the needs of the people. And those of you transitioning to adulthood are the most vulnerable in society. You are who Arcis wishes to keep safe, to protect from outside influences.'

The supervisor gestured at the bed. 'Back in bed, Mr Pavesi. While it has been interesting chatting with you, I must get on with other things. Lights out in five minutes.'

The supervisor left and Dom pulled the curtain closed around his bed. He sat on the edge of his cot. The supervisor had mentioned the Collective. Was that a council that controlled Praesidium? He slipped back under the covers just as the lights went out.

His mother had been trapped in this place. Was she ever on this floor? Did she lie in this exact same bed?

The Rebels

Carlo appeared in his mind's eye. What he'd done to his father had been to protect his mother.

It had been easy luring Carlo out to the woods. All he had to do was tell him about a store of drink buried in some shallow grave. His piece-of-shit father had come stumbling through the forest, but Dom hadn't prepared for his mother to be with him, or for Carlo to be stone-cold sober.

Carlo had his hand curled into Mariella's hair. His other fist was red. A trail of blood snaked down his mother's face. The asshole had broken her nose.

'A little collateral, son.'

Dom hated it when he called him that.

'You're getting a little too old for my hand, these days. But she'—Carlo walked Mariella closer—'is easier to control, especially when I threaten you.'

'Let her go!' said Dom.

'Dom...' breathed Mariella. 'Don't listen to him.'

'Shut up!' Carlo pinched her broken nose. She squealed so loud that Dom hoped the town's residents would hear it. But he'd purposely picked a place far from the town and in the middle of nowhere, to confront his father and convince him to leave. Now he wished for a more public place.

'It was all too convenient that you'd find the exact thing I would kill for, out here, in a remote place where nobody was around.' Carlo smiled. 'Don't think I didn't know what you had planned.'

'Let her go,' repeated Dom. He'd been secretly working out, bulking up. Not only to distance himself from his ugly scars, but to prepare for the day he would take on his father.

Carlo pushed Mariella to the ground. She groaned and quickly added, 'I'm okay.'

Dom was glad she did. He'd been about to go to her.

'You know,' said Carlo, 'Praesidium was prepared to give me anything I wanted for you. They liked how the surgeries went, said you had "responsive tissue regeneration". Whatever the hell that means. Because I remember breaking all your fingers one time and they didn't heal that fast.' He laughed. 'But I struggled to give you up because you were blood. And this one...' He spat at Mariella. 'This one said I should give you a chance to change. But I feel like giving you exactly what you gave me, which is a big fat nothing.'

Mariella looked up at Dom with soft, pained eyes. She shook her head at him.

A warning.

Dom's fast breaths tightened his chest. He clenched his hands, sick of making excuses for this man. But no more. He was no longer the kid who blamed himself for the beatings, some of which he took for his mother. His father was a human incapable of seeing past his own shit. And for that, the man needed to be gone.

'I can get you drink,' said Dom. 'Anything you want. If you leave Foxrush now and never come back.'

Carlo laughed. 'Now why would I do that, *son*, when I have everything I want right here.'

'Because if you don't go, I'll kill you.'

Carlo laughed harder. 'You might be eighteen, Dominic, but you're no match for me. Your puny muscles are fine if you're going a few rounds with a girl. By the way, how's Sheila doing? Quite the looker she's grown up to be.' He licked his lips.

Dom growled. Talking about Sheila was off limits.

He ran at Carlo and hit him mid-waist. Carlo grunted and hit the ground hard. Dom jumped to his feet, breathing hard, ready for a counterattack, but when one never came he straightened up. His father lay on the ground, blood seeping from a cut on his head. His open eyes were cold, glassy.

Mariella crawled forward and pressed two shaky fingers to his neck. She stood up and leaned against a tree for support.

'He's dead.'

Dom backed off, raked his hands through his hair. 'No... no! I didn't mean to...'

Her eyes were on Carlo and the rock that his head had struck.

'Shh,' she said, and pulled him into a hug. 'Now, listen to me very carefully. I need you to go back to Foxrush and get a few things.' She whispered them in his ear. 'We're going to bury him so deep it will take team of archaeologists to find him.'

Dom shook the memory away and settled beneath the grey covers in the hospital ward. The only way to release his guilt would be to find his mother. That meant playing Arcis' game and cutting off contact with anyone who risked his progress, including Anya.

11

'Sheila, I can't do this anymore. I need to sleep.'

'We don't have a choice. We have to stay awake.'

It was midnight in Arcis and both the ground- and first-floor activities had shut down for the night. But the higher floors operated at odd hours. He and Sheila slumped on their beds in the second floor dorm. The overhead light remained on. He wore a white boiler suit, which was peeled down to his waist. Thirty-six hours of being awake, with nothing but snatched moments of sleep thrown in, was taking its toll.

In some screwed up way, he missed the first floor. Both Sheila and Dom had made rotation. Brianna hadn't been so lucky. A lump formed in his throat when he thought about how he'd used her.

The second floor had brought with it its own mysteries. The instant they stepped out of the elevator, a supervisor had handed them a first-aid book and showed them a three-minute video on how to do CPR. Dom and Sheila were now the official on-call medics along with several other untrained teenagers.

Dom closed his eyes. The overhead light bled through his eyelids. He draped an arm over the orange hue, hoping another emergency wouldn't happen for an hour. That's all he needed. His body gave in to the heaviness of sleep.

But the female supervisor's warnings about tardiness being linked to punishment kept his mind from shutting off. He'd shared those warnings with Sheila after the supervisor released him from hospital. She couldn't figure out this place either. What punishment would they receive if he or Sheila slept through an emergency call?

There were eight others in the communal sleeping area, all in various states of undress. Dom felt bone tired and weary. He wasn't sure how much more he could take. With his brain running on a quarter capacity, it was only a matter of time before he made a mistake.

The overhead lights still stung his eyes, even with his arm blocking it out. The bed felt soft enough that he forgot about the illumination. An intermittent buzzing noise sounded, and suddenly he was awake again.

Sleep deprivation and how to cope with it. That must be the lesson on the second floor.

His body sank further into the mattress. He felt his mind switching off, drifting into another consciousness. Then a voice shrilled over the loudspeaker.

'Dom and Sheila, you're needed on the fourth floor.'

Sheila bolted upright in the bed next to his. 'What the...' She touched a hand to her head.

Dom sat up and fed his arms lazily into the top half of his boiler suit. He stood and pulled the zip up halfway. A green box with a white cross sat on the floor next to his bed. He groped for it and shuffled to the exit.

Sheila yawned as they rode the elevator up to the fourth floor. There were three medical prefabs in Tower A, in the room beyond the changing room. Neither Dom nor

Sheila was allowed to see the activities of any floor they had yet to reach. The prefabs were as far as the medics were allowed to go.

The elevator doors opened and a guttural scream—low and persistent—stopped Dom cold.

'What the hell was that?' said Sheila.

He stepped out into the changing room. His foot slipped on something wet. He looked down to see drops of blood leading from the elevator to the next room.

Dom jogged to the exit and pushed the door open. Beyond was a trio of prefabs set next to each other in a large open space. The light shone at half the level of the one in his sleeping quarters. A pool of blood shimmered in a spot close to the open door of one of the prefabs, as if someone had bled out.

More screams, deep and tortured, came from inside the prefab. He shook off his remaining lethargy and picked up the pace.

Breathe, Pavesi.

'It's probably just a flesh wound,' he said. 'We know how to deal with those.' Sheila kept pace with him, carrying her own medical box.

The worst emergency between them so far was an electric-shock victim from the first floor.

She flashed him a sceptical look. 'You ever scream like that from a flesh wound?'

They climbed up the few steps and inside the prefab. Sitting on the bed was a wide-eyed girl, her mouth open and frozen. A panicked boy stood beside her, holding her left arm up above her head. The blood-soaked bandage around her wrist worried Dom.

'Thank God you're here!' said the boy. 'I didn't know what else to do. She's lost a lot of blood.'

'What happened?' said Sheila.

'There was a door with a saw. It... it came out of nowhere. She managed to slip her hand out of the handle in time, but the saw caught her just above the wrist.'

Dom looked at Sheila. 'What do we do?'

She shrugged.

The boy looked from Sheila to Dom. 'You mean you don't know?' He let the girl's arm drop. She screamed with pain.

Focus, Pavesi. What do we do first? His brain refused to cooperate. Snippets from the first-aid book came back to him.

'Hold that arm up,' he snapped. 'Higher than her heart.'

The frightened boy did as he was told.

Using sanitising gel from the boxes, Dom and Sheila cleaned their hands. The boy strained to keep the injury elevated. Tears streamed down the girl's blotchy face. Her chest heaved with sobs.

Dom whispered to Sheila. 'Can you keep her calm while I think about what to do?'

She dried her hands on her boiler suit. 'We have to stop the bleeding first. Then we need to give her a shot of morphine for the pain.'

Of course. He would have figured that out if he weren't so tired.

'Look at me,' said Sheila to the girl. 'I want you to focus on my face. We're going to help you, but I need you to stay calm. Dom's going to give you something for the pain, but first we have to stop the bleeding.'

When Dom peeled back the bandage from the girl's arm, he saw the blood flow had been stemmed. 'She didn't nick an artery, so that's a good start. Lie her down and keep the arm elevated.'

Sheila eased her into a lying position and held her

arm up. The girl whimpered. She couldn't have been more than sixteen.

'I tried to pull her away, but I wasn't fast enough,' said the boy, stepping back from the table. 'God, look at her...'

'That's not helping,' said Sheila. 'If you're going to stand there and make useless comments, then go.'

The boy backed out of the room. 'Yeah, I think that's best. Sorry.'

The door to the prefab rattled when he slammed it.

'He wasn't helping much, anyway,' said Sheila to the terrified girl. Dom handed her a square of gauze.

She pressed the gauze into the gash just above her wrist. It had cut down to the bone. 'The good news is it's a clean cut.'

The girl bucking and writhing in pain didn't agree. Dom prepared the morphine dosage.

'We need to close the wound, Dom. Fast. It's going to get infected.'

A small screen on the wall activated when he waved his chip over it. It contained information on the types of equipment Arcis had, but nothing about procedures. He searched for ways to deal with a deep cut. He found a picture of a photo medicine machine that would heal the wound through use of light therapy. He looked around and found the machine attached to the prefab's wall. It had an arm with a tapered end.

Dom pulled the arm out from the wall and turned the machine on. He positioned the tapered end over the girl's wound. Light pulsed over the area and the wound started to knit closed. He applied a spray-on bandage containing an antibiotic ointment.

Finally, he prepared an IV drip with morphine and fed it into a vein on the girl's other arm. After ten minutes, she was falling asleep.

'What the hell's going on in this place?' said Dom. 'How are kids winding up with near amputations? She's lucky she didn't lose her hand.'

'It was probably just an accident. One of the other floors. We don't know what's going on.'

'You really believe that?'

Sheila shook her head. 'But we have no other explanation.'

The door opened and the female supervisor came in. 'Have you successfully treated the girl's wound?'

'Yeah,' said Dom. 'What happened to her? She lost a lot of blood.'

The supervisor ignored Dom and leaned over the girl. She checked the wound and tilted the arm in various directions. At least the girl was out for it.

'And you used the photo medicine machine and the spray-on bandage?'

'Yes, like the screen instructed.'

The female supervisor clicked her fingers and the male supervisor from the first floor appeared at the door. He joined her and together they inspected the wound.

'Good closure. Don't you agree, One?'

'Yes, it seems to have left minimal scarring, Two. We need to move her.'

'Where are you taking her?' said Sheila.

'Somewhere she will be more comfortable,' said the male supervisor. 'Thank you for your assistance in this matter. You can go back to your dorm after you've cleaned the room and the blood from the floor outside.'

'Wait!' said Dom. 'What about this machine? I've never seen it repair wounds so fast. What is it? Where did it come from?'

'Praesidium tech. A prototype.'

The male supervisor lifted the girl into his arms while the female detached the machine from the holder on the wall and collected what was left of the spray-on bandage. 'From now on you will learn how to suture. This machine is no longer available for use.'

The two supervisors exited the room, careful to avoid stepping in the blood. 'Why?' Sheila called after them. She turned to Dom. 'Where are they taking her?'

He leaned against the edge of the table. 'I don't know. Close the door.'

He'd already checked the prefabs for cameras and was certain there weren't any.

Sheila did.

'I can't do this,' he said. 'I want out.'

Sheila stared at him. 'We can't leave. We need to see this to the end. It's not just about you.'

'Let Max send someone else in here to replace us. This is getting dangerous. Kids are almost losing limbs now. When did that happen?' He rubbed his eyes. 'I'm so goddamn tired I can barely think straight. I just... I can't...'

Sheila gripped his hands. 'Dom, look at me. It's just the lack of sleep talking. We're in this until the end. There's no leaving. You get that, right? There's only one way out of this hellhole. Arcis won't let us walk out.'

Dom pushed her away and found a scalpel. 'Watch me.' He poised it over the spot on his wrist where his chip was implanted.

Sheila lunged for him and snatched the scalpel out of his hand. 'Don't! What can I say to make this okay for you?'

Dom sank back against the bed. 'There's nothing you can say to talk me out of it. I'm leaving.'

'What about Anya?'

Dom perked up. 'What about her?'

'You're going to leave her to tackle this place on her own?'

Shit. He hadn't thought about that.

'She'll be fine.'

'No, she won't. She needs you. And I'm starting to realise you need her, too.' Sheila sighed. 'I can't believe I'm about to suggest this, but you've been threatening to tell her about us for weeks. I think you should.'

Dom stared at her. 'Why now?'

'Maybe you're right. Maybe we need allies in here. June's on the floor below, but Anya, well, you two seem to motivate each other. So, yeah, tell her. But only her.'

'Are you sure?'

'If it'll help to focus your butt, then I'm all for it. I can't do this alone. I won't.'

He pulled Sheila into a hug. 'Thanks.'

She pushed him away gently. 'Yeah, well, I'm still on the fence about her. So you'd better see something in her I haven't.'

They turned their attention to the mess in the room. Dom used his new burst of energy to good effect while it lasted. As he cleaned, he thought about ways to tell Anya his secret. What would her reaction be?

Before he said anything, he would need to give her one thing. It was tucked away in a secret compartment of his bag.

The antidote to Compliance.

12

Twenty steps from the bathroom to the suspended walkway.

Fifteen steps across to the other side.

Twenty-five steps through the empty room in Tower A to the changing room.

Ten steps from the changing room to the elevator.

A total of seventy steps from his location on the second floor to the lobby and freedom.

But his access card for the elevator stopped working last night and no longer gave him access to the ground floor. He and Sheila were trapped inside Arcis. Even if he wanted to escape he couldn't.

A large infirmary dominated the area in Tower B on the second floor. Dom knew it well when he'd spent a few days there after receiving a severe shock. But what he hadn't noticed before was its segregation from the mixed dorms. Both he and Sheila worked as first aiders, yet neither of them had permission to enter the infirmary, except as patients.

But Dom had more pressing problems than the secrecy of the infirmary—his lack of sleep for one. Then last night, a miracle happened. No emergencies to wake for, no blood to clean up. Six hours of uninterrupted sleep.

It had happened just after Dom had stopped yet another teenager from bleeding out. This time it was a boy from the second floor who'd tended to an emergency only to slice his finger open on a scalpel in his medical kit. After Dom had stopped the bleeding and wrapped it, he demanded to speak to a supervisor. When the female supervisor finally decided to show, he'd shown her the room full of zombie-like teenagers who could barely stand, let alone tend to medical emergencies.

'We're not machines,' he'd said. 'We need sleep. We've already had an accident on this floor. A boy sliced his finger open. That wouldn't have happened if he'd been rested.'

The supervisor had looked at him as if to say 'So?', but then she spoke to someone unseen and unheard. 'Arcis will consider this. Stay in the dorm and remain on-call.'

That morning, Dom enjoyed his new clarity as he stood next to Sheila in the shared bathroom. Tactics and strategy had been all but forgotten on the second floor. He didn't know how long the good feeling would last, or if Arcis would change their mind.

With just the two of them in the room, Dom admired his short hair in the mirror. He'd expected to see Carlo after the cut, but he only saw traces of the man who'd worn a permanent scowl. When Dom completed all nine of Arcis' floors and got out of here, he would take Charlie up on his offer and get his hair cut properly.

Sheila pulled at the skin around her eyes. 'Thank God. The dark circles are going away. I thought I might have to get some drastic procedure done when I got out of here. I'm too young for crow's feet or bags. What you said to the supervisor last night must have worked. They're not sharp enough to think of that all by themselves.'

She'd meant it as a joke, but Dom had noticed the supervisors' lack of empathy long before their arrival on the second floor. It was almost like they didn't understand how fragile teenagers could be.

'Have you made a note of the exits on this floor, and how many cameras there are?' said Dom.

He was certain there weren't any cameras in the bathroom, but not why.

He'd counted two in the dorm, four in the infirmary. There were two in the changing room where the elevator was, and one in the elevator itself.

The people who ran this programme were watching them, recording and monitoring them. For Arcis? Or was it for the mysterious "Collective" in Praesidium?

'Relax, Dom. You're too wound up. They've cut off our access to the outside. We're not going anywhere. Why don't we just see what happens?'

The thought rattled him. The supervisors spoke with mystery voices who whispered in their ear. 'I can't sit back and do nothing. It feels like we're missing things we should be seeing.'

He thought about the supervisors: one male on the first floor, one female on the second. Both had shown up when the girl with the near amputation had almost bled out. Both had seemed detached, aloof. Both had cared little for the safety of the participants who put themselves in harm's way. He would tell Max about how unfeeling the supervisors were the next time he got a message to the outside. But other than their lack of empathy, what was so unusual about them? Or the Collective, the female supervisor had mentioned, who ran this place? How would that information assist Max or Charlie in their plans to shut down Arcis?

The only noteworthy development so far was a dip

in the brightness of the lights, just before rotation.

'We could go round in circles trying to figure out the point of everything,' said Sheila, touching a finger to her brow. 'The answers will come, when you stop thinking so hard about it.'

'I told you something was up with the first floor, especially after the last shock killed Brianna. But you wouldn't listen,' he said. 'I feel like we're missing some key component about this place.'

He didn't like to think about the girl on the first floor, or how easily, after two weeks of constant running, the group had turned on the slowest and weakest member. The supervisor had promised them all rotation if they sacrificed the slowest. Dom had reached his limit of shocks. But he hadn't expected the last shock Brianna received to be the one that killed her.

Sheila sighed. 'Even if we'd known about it, what Arcis was willing to do, could we have saved Brianna? They had it in for her. If it wasn't her, it would have been someone else. Stop worrying about things you can't control.'

Dom had heard the male and female supervisor talking on the first floor about how those controlling Arcis needed to move things on. He'd expected Compliance to act as a buffer and protect Brianna from the severity of the shocks; up until now, they'd been harmless enough. But when the shock that hit Brianna wouldn't stop, Dom knew this time was different. Sheila had almost died separating the girl from the conduit. As soon as she had, the electricity stopped.

Arcis had changed him, made him cold and hard like the supervisors. He'd sacrificed Brianna to better his own situation.

Or maybe killing his father had changed him.

Dom turned and leaned his hands against the sink.

'What's wrong?' said Sheila. 'You've got that look in your eye.'

'This whole situation is messed up. It was so easy for us to use others to get what we wanted.'

Sheila turned and mirrored his stance. '*Use* others? What about what Arcis is doing to us? You think this sleep deprivation is a necessity? You think the accidents are avoidable? Because I do. A girl almost lost her hand. Either the participants are being put into situations they can't handle, or they haven't read Arcis' safety manual.'

Dom folded his arms. 'I don't like who I'm becoming.'

'What? An impulsive, stubborn control freak who is also the most caring man I know?' She pushed him gently. 'Get away from me, you freak.'

Dom laughed despite his mood. 'I'm serious.'

'So am I. We're doing our best in here, Dom. We can't let this place get the better of us.'

'It already has.'

'What do you mean?'

'My father. I'm becoming like him.'

Sheila pushed him harder, punched his arm a couple of times. 'Listen to me, Dom. You are nothing like that lying, drunk, violent sack of crap. And I never want to hear you talk about yourself in that way again. You hear me?'

Dom avoided her gaze.

'Do. You. Hear. Me?'

'I killed him, Sheila. That already makes me like him. He would have done the same to me, to my mother. But I think he enjoyed torturing all of us.'

'You didn't kill him,' Sheila whispered. 'He stumbled and split his head open.'

'Because I pushed him.'

'Because he was hurting your mother. You were protecting her.' Sheila stepped away and released a breath. 'He made a pass at me, you know.'

He gripped the sink. 'When?'

'About three months before he died. I was looking for you. You and Mariella were out. He invited me in. Asked if I wanted a drink. I said no. Then he pinned me against the wall, told me I was sexy.' She shuddered.

He pushed off from the sink, his hands two fists. 'Jesus, Sheila. Why didn't you tell me? What did that bastard do?'

'Nothing. He was unsteady, already drunk. I managed to slip away, get the hell out of there.'

Dom remembered it now: her refusal to live in the house. She never said why. His stomach swirled thinking about what might have happened, what he hadn't noticed. He groped for the sink to steady himself. Why hadn't he paid attention?

'It wasn't the first time, either,' said Sheila. 'He used to look at me funny when I was younger. I just ignored him.'

'I'm so sorry, Sheila. I didn't know.'

'It wasn't your fault. Yours or Mariella's. He was a control freak, had to have everything his way.'

'I guess I inherited one of his traits. That and impulsiveness.'

Sheila stepped forward and cupped his face. Her eyes shimmered. 'But everything you do is with love in your heart. He didn't have a heart. Never compare yourself to him again.'

Dom nodded and she kissed him on the cheek.

They left the bathroom together and waited in the dormitory for the next emergency. Ten minutes later, the first call of the day came in. Dom and Sheila dealt with three mild shocks from the fifth floor, two attempted suicides from the fourth and a deep cut from the third. The suicides worried him the most. Were the participants really under that much stress?

What happened on the fourth floor that the participants considered taking their own lives?

Ω

He'd done it. He'd given Anya the antidote. A few days ago she'd received her first shock. He'd been first on the scene and tended to her. While she was disorientated, he'd given her the medicine that helped to control arrhythmia after an electric shock. The medicine had one extra ingredient: Charlie's antidote. Dom had tried to visit her in the infirmary, but his access card refused him admission.

How was she feeling? Was she confused, angry, irritated? Compliance smothered emotions. The antidote released them. The dominant feeling to return differed in everyone. For Dom it had been uncontrollable anger. He'd almost broken his hand punching the outside walls of Charlie and Max's bungalow.

Soon Anya would see Arcis for what it wasn't—the sanctuary it pretended to be. Maybe she'd see something different to him. Arcis was pulling them deeper into a programme that tested them psychologically.

Why? He didn't know. But he needed Anya to help him figure it out.

Giving her the antidote had ignited a new fear inside him. It brought him one step closer to telling her what he was.

She must understand he had no choice. The rebellion had to happen. Her parents had to die.

Would she yell and scream, accuse him of using her? He wouldn't blame her if she did. Who in their right mind would want to befriend a killer?

Yet, he had to take the risk. She had something he lacked, something that might give him the edge in this place of lies. Sheila gave him strength, but Anya understood his loneliness in ways Sheila never could.

Anya was the light at the end of a long, dark tunnel. Around her, he felt peace. Dom hadn't felt that since before the age of seven, when a team of doctors first cut him open.

13

The female supervisor burst into the second floor dormitories. 'Everyone get up! Now. Rotation is imminent.'

Dom shielded his face from the overhead lights. What time was it? He'd been working late last night trying to remember how to reset a broken arm. He'd fallen into bed only a few minutes earlier.

He checked his watch. Nope. Two hours ago.

Dom kicked off the covers and placed his feet on the floor, groaning and scrubbing his scalp. In the bed next to him, Sheila looked more alert, but not by much.

The supervisor hovered close to the door. 'Stand by your beds, now.'

Eleven participants lined up, in various states of awake and undress. Boiler suits half on, half off, they watched the floor with heavy-lidded eyes.

The supervisor wrinkled her nose at the dishevelled appearances. 'The left side of the room will rotate today. The rest of you will continue on the second floor.'

She turned and strode out of the dormitory. Only four on Dom's side of the room had made rotation.

He dressed fast and fired his possessions into his

backpack, before the supervisor came back and changed her mind

'Thank God,' said Sheila. 'Can't say I'll miss this floor.'

They waited by the elevator with the other two who'd rotated, Lucas and Lilly. Nobody spoke. Dom needed at least another six hours of sleep before he could formulate words. The elevator whirred as it came from the floor below. The doors opened; a brown-haired boy waited inside. They climbed in and mumbled greetings to him.

Dom stared at the ground while the elevator took them one floor up. The doors opened and he exited into an identical changing room to the one on the floor below. They weren't alone. A girl waited, judging by her grey-and-white trainers. He shuffled into the room, unable to look up at her. Sheila jabbed him in the arm with her finger, but tiredness made it difficult to muster any interest.

He heard a familiar voice say, 'I just left you!'

His heart pounded out a new rhythm and looked up to see Anya. Her eyes were less dilated. She appeared sharper and more alert to how he remembered her being on the ground floor. She was staring at the brown-haired boy.

He'd heard a rumour that a few days ago someone from the second floor had treated a girl called Tahlia Odare, but she'd died. Tahlia had lived in Praesidium before being returned to the towns. Not many people escaped the city and June had been sent in to Arcis to find out more about her.

He'd also heard another rumour that Tahlia had suffered the same fate as Brianna, and Anya had almost died separating her from the scanner. If he wasn't so tired he would have told her what an idiot she'd been. In the back of his mind, he worried that Arcis had targeted

Tahlia, possibly because she'd lived in Praesidium.

'I know,' said the boy smiling. 'Supervisor One came to get me when you left. He sent me to the second floor. Jerome nearly had a heart attack. But then Supervisor Two sent me to this floor. And here I am.'

Dom stared at the new boy. Had he heard him right? Why had Arcis changed the rules and allowed him to skip a floor?

Anya flicked her eyes to Dom, then away. Dom couldn't even manage a hello. After he slept, they would talk.

He managed quick introductions all round, then passed a tight-lipped Anya to get to the clothes rail. He was being a jerk. But her presence on this floor had shocked him into silence.

Everyone dressed fast. Dom yawned into his fist. 'I'm going to need some sleep before I fall down.'

The others followed him as he made his way across the suspended walkway connecting Tower A and B. He entered a poorly lit room in Tower B to see a wall ahead of him with three openings, each marked by a different colour above the opening: blue, green and black. Three separate sconces lit up each entrance point. He found a small screen by the exit door containing a rudimentary map of the room: the blue section was the dorm and the green section was the kitchen. The black section had no listing.

Dom headed for the dorm. All except Anya followed him. As he walked away, his skin tightened at the new awkwardness between them. In his mind, he turned around and told her they would talk soon. In reality, he kept walking.

Dom dropped onto a bed three away from the entrance to the dorm. He must have passed out because the next thing he heard was movement in the room. The others were awake.

Rubbing his eyes, he sat up. 'What time is it?'

'Midday,' said Sheila. 'We've been asleep for three hours. We're going to explore. You coming?'

Three hours had taken the edge off his mood. He got up, still dressed in his new clothes: a bottle-green hoodie and grey trousers. He looked around the room that was painted in a royal blue; the grey ceiling and grey bedspreads provided the only colour contrast. The constricting feel of the dark walls sent a shiver through him. 'Yeah, sounds like a good idea.'

As he marched back to the open area, his stomach clenched at the thought of seeing Anya again. She was free of Compliance. Would she still want to be his friend? How would he begin to explain what he and Sheila were?

He exited the blue section and entered the middle one, arriving at a kitchen and a communal room. Anya was asleep on one of the beanbags dotted around the communal space. Smiling, he hunkered down to her level and shook her gently.

'Wakey, wakey.'

Her eyelids fluttered open, and his heart skipped a little when she flashed her cobalt-blue eyes at him.

She crawled forward and climbed to her feet. 'How long have I been asleep?' Anya stiffened when her gaze flickered to a spot behind him.

Sheila.

Too much had happened on the second floor for Dom to keep up the pretence. It was bad enough Arcis was playing them. He didn't need to do it to people he liked.

'A few hours. Not sure. There aren't any clocks in here.' Dom looked around. 'Did the supervisor come?'

Anya shook her head.

A piece of hair stuck out at an angle from Anya's head. He smiled and reached out for it. Anya blushed red and fixed the issue before he could.

'So, are we still pretending, Dom?' said Sheila. 'Or can I drop the charade now?'

Dom gritted his teeth. 'Not now.'

'Because I thought the plan was to get her this far. And now here she is.'

'I *said*, not now.'

'What are you two talking about?' said Anya. Her eyes flicked between them.

'Nothing,' said Dom. 'Just Sheila shooting her mouth off.'

He glared at Sheila one last time.

'Okay. You're the boss.'

He was going to kill her.

Anya chewed on her lip in a way that Dom liked. But she was unsure, hesitant. And he knew why.

'I, uh, I'm sorry about Tahlia.'

Anya dropped her head and hid behind a veil of hair. 'Thanks.' He would ask her about it properly when Sheila wasn't around.

With nothing to do but explore, the group of six navigated their way back to the exit and checked the map that showed a maze with three parts. Dom divided everyone up into two teams of two; he and Sheila agreed to split up so they could cover the maze faster. He concentrated on the only part yet to be explored: the black section. Anya had said she'd checked out the section and found nothing, but he wouldn't be happy until he'd checked every corridor and seen every turn for himself.

A second look wouldn't hurt. Maybe she'd missed something.

Dom exhausted his route, but Sheila had better luck.

They regrouped and discovered a glossy gold door at the back of the black section. Should they open it, should they wait?

Something told him this was a test. Until he knew more about what the controllers had set up here, they would wait.

An hour into a darts tournament back in the communal section, partly to let off steam, partly to distract Lucas and Frank from the door, the novelty of it wore off.

Sheila led the boys back to the screen at the entrance, to see if she could find out more about their purpose here. He trusted her to keep them in line. Last thing he needed was someone going rogue and ruining their chances of getting out.

Anya stayed back, as did Lilly. Lilly stuck on a pair of headphones and tuned him and Anya out.

He swallowed. The talk he didn't want to have, but secretly did, had come. This could go one of two ways.

A bout of nerves hit him and made him feel sick.

She wore her hesitance like a second skin. He hated this distance between them and he worried that lack of Compliance had made her less open to friendship.

'So,' she said, 'what was life like on the second floor?'

Those nine words lifted the heaviness from the room.

They chatted for a while. To Dom's relief, their ease with each other wasn't a Compliance fluke. Maybe Anya would take his other news well. But first, he needed to ask her about Tahlia. From her quiet demeanour, he could tell the event had shaken her.

'You're different,' he said.

'Yeah, so are you.'

Her answer surprised him. Maybe he *had* changed.

Maybe he had enough of pretending in this place. The only person he cared for other than Sheila was sitting on the beanbag next to him. He wanted to tell her everything. But with cameras in the room, he had to keep the conversation light.

'How are you?' said Dom. 'You know, after Tahlia?'

'I'm still shaking.'

'I'm sorry I couldn't see you after, you know, when she died. I asked, but the supervisor wouldn't let me.' A nervous laugh bubbled up and out. He folded his arms. 'I even tried to pretend it was part of some routine check-up.'

He'd also tried to see Tahlia. The access pad to the infirmary had flashed red when he'd tried his floor card. So he'd offered his assistance. But when the supervisor said it wouldn't be necessary, he suspected Tahlia had been targeted.

Maybe June would shed light on the mysterious girl who'd once lived in Praesidium.

He and Anya chatted about what happened. He could see it upset her to talk about it, but he needed to ask her why she disconnected Tahlia from the terminal alone. Sheila had done the same thing with Brianna and had almost died.

'It was dangerous, Anya. You could have been killed.'

'I can handle myself.'

'You need to be careful in here.' He grazed the top of her hand with his fingers, watching for her reaction. '*I* need you to be careful.'

She snatched her hand away and stared at him.

'It was my fault, okay? Is that what you want me to say? I killed Tahlia. It was my fault.' He reached for her again but she jerked away from him. 'I felt guilty. That's why I helped.'

He hated seeing her like this, under a stress that was of Arcis' making. He laced his hand in hers and felt her relax a little. Then, he told her about Brianna, about how the first-floor participants had targeted her because she was the slowest.

'Was it you?'

Her accusation surprised him and he looked away. 'It was all of us. We were set up.' He looked back. 'It wasn't your fault and it wasn't ours. And I'm guessing you didn't come up with the idea all on your own.'

She shook her head.

He wanted to hold her, to tell her she wasn't alone. But she still believed the rebels had murdered her parents. It was a lie Praesidium had spread among the towns and it would be hard to convince her otherwise.

'I went back the next night, after the self-defence classes,' said Anya. 'But you weren't there.'

His lips parted in surprise. He'd forgotten about promising to show her more moves. The first-floor gauntlets had kept his mind occupied, not to mention the shocks. Dom leaned back and took a moment to really look at her. Not stolen glances or distracted chats over lunch. Her lips were slightly parted. Her throat bobbed as she swallowed. His gaze lifted to meet her inquisitive eyes. A tear rolled down her cheek. Before he could stop himself, he thumbed it away. Anya drew in a quick breath.

'Arcis forced me to stay after my first shock,' he said. 'Then Sheila was shocked the next day.'

Anya tensed and pulled her hand out of his. He missed the warmth of her fingers. These stolen moments weren't enough for him. Did she feel the same things for him as he felt for her?

'I don't know what's going on with you two, but I

don't want to get in the middle of something.'

'Yeah, I wanted to explain about that...'

The others returned and cut his time with Anya short. While they all sat and talked, the first thought he'd had since arriving on this floor hit him full force. Why had Anya and Frank skipped the second floor?

14

Arcis knew how to do boredom well. Dom and the others had been on the third floor for nearly twelve hours. No supervisor had come. They took turns napping in case one did.

It was close to midnight when Anya called it a night. Dom wished her pleasant dreams.

His sleep cycle was all over the place, and while he knew he should turn in too, the urge to explore more overruled his body. He started with the communal space and kitchen and spent a few minutes cataloguing the layout of the rooms. He opened cupboards, pulled out plates and cups, pulled the dartboard off the wall. Nothing. He examined the section with the headphones.

Everything looked normal.

Tiredness hit him and he made a strong cup of coffee. On the way back to the dorm, Dom checked over every wall in the blue section of the maze. Finding nothing out of place bothered him. The walls felt sturdy when he touched them, the floor cold beneath his stockinged feet. As he pressed his gaze into every blue panel, one thing he couldn't find were the cameras he was sure Arcis had hidden.

If he couldn't find the cameras, he couldn't work out the location of the blind spots.

He made it to the entrance of the bathroom when he stumbled, jerked upright, and spilled the coffee over him. The mug dropped from his fingers and rolled across the floor, unbroken.

A fire dragged across his skin. He hissed and stumbled into the bathroom. It wasn't empty, as he had hoped. Anya was there.

Shit.

He muttered his apologies. A shocked Anya stared at him, at the stain on his T-shirt. There was no time to explain.

His skin pulsated with heat as he groped for the cold tap and turned it on. He yanked up his T-shirt, gathered handfuls of water and splashed them on his skin. He let out a long sigh as the cool water cancelled out the raging fire.

His shirt was still up when he heard Anya pull in a sharp breath. *Double shit.* Only one thing would cause her to draw breath like that: the C-shaped scar he'd got when doctors in Praesidium removed one of his lungs. He'd been sick as a child and Praesidium had been the only place with the technology and medical knowledge to fix him. He yanked his shirt down, but it was too late. Why hadn't he used the sink in the kitchen?

Because this one was the closest.

Dom avoided her gaze. He'd worked so hard to hide his scars; they weakened him and he didn't want to see her disgust.

She would have found out eventually, Dom. Why not tell her?

No. He wasn't ready to relive the pain of his childhood.

He bolted from the room and almost knocked Sheila

over.

'Where are you off to?' said Sheila.

'Nowhere. I'm going to bed.'

Sheila knew exactly what Praesidium and their medical teams had done to him. She was the only person who knew how much he hated his scars. But she would take his secret to the grave. As he opened the door to the dorm room, he glanced behind to see Sheila enter the bathroom. What would Anya ask her? What would Sheila say?

His heart pounded too loudly in his chest. With shaky hands, he removed his soiled T-shirt and pulled on a fresh one before crawling into bed. The smell of coffee lingered in the air. He pretended to be asleep when Sheila, then Anya, came in. As soon as they had settled, he flipped onto his back and stared into the darkness.

His surgery was a day he would never forget. His mother had been fussing over him, while his father had been nervous about something, but not so nervous he couldn't flirt with a couple of the nurses.

Dom had just turned seven when he'd started to feel ill. Shortness of breath came first, and then a too-fast heartbeat that felt like someone was sitting on his chest. His parents had contacted Praesidium. The next day, a team came to get him and brought him to the city. Doctors there diagnosed Dom with pneumothorax, or a collapsed lung. It took three days for them to re-inflate his lung. After, they sent him home. But the same thing happened again and again, until a lung replacement became the only long-term option for Dom.

Then his kidneys failed next. In one year, Dom had lost a lung, a kidney and part of his liver.

Mariella had tried to be strong, but even she'd struggled with his sickness. Carlo had been fascinated with the finer details of the surgery, rather than the welfare of his son. After each surgery and like clockwork, Carlo would disappear for a month to return a sober, changed man. He was attentive to Mariella; he even spent time with Dom. Then in a week, he would revert back to his old drunken habits. Dom had almost looked forward to the next surgery.

He'd learned to live with the loss of a lung. While it hampered his ability to run, his consistent training helped him to overcome any shortfalls in his fitness. His scars had become a hot topic at school. That's when he'd met Sheila, a loud, sweary girl who had everybody in the palm of her hand.

He was eleven when one bully ordered Dom to lay face-down in a mud patch. He was half way to the ground when Sheila appeared and began kicking and punching the boy until he gave up and left. Without a word, she pulled Dom to his feet. He stood there, staring at her, shocked into silence.

'Are you okay?' she said

He brushed the mud off his trousers. 'Yeah.'

'What happened to you?' She was pointing to his lung scar.

Dom yanked his top down. 'Nothing.'

'Doesn't look like nothing to me.'

'Thanks for your help.' He walked away but she followed him.

'Hey, what's your name?'

He glanced back at her. She was a pretty girl with brown hair and sun-kissed golden streaks. 'Dominic. Why?'

'Mine's Sheila. How about we stick together, Dom?'

He faced the front. 'No thanks. I don't fit in with

your crowd. And my name's Dominic, not Dom.'

She walked alongside him. 'Well, I prefer Dom. And who said they were my crowd?'

He flashed her a sceptical look.

'Okay, so I hang around with them, but that's a survival thing.' She rolled her eyes. 'I prefer you to them, anyway. I think you and I should be friends.'

She linked her arm through his.

He tried to pull his arm away. 'I don't need a friend.'

That only made her grip harder. 'I wasn't asking, Dom...'

A noise in the dorm broke him from his reverie. He sat up and noticed both Anya's and Frank's beds were empty. His first thought hit him in the stomach hard. There was only one place they might go.

He scrambled out of bed and shook Sheila from her sleep. She mumbled something rude under her breath.

'Sheila, wake up!' he whispered.

'What, Dom? Just let me sleep.'

'You have to come, now. I think Frank and Anya are about to do something stupid.'

15

There was only one girl in Arcis, besides Sheila, who made Dom's blood run hot. He'd almost lost her to the game on the third. He and Sheila had raced through the black section to discover her covered in blood. Frank's blood. He hadn't made it.

In the prefab, Anya sat on the edge of the bed, numb from the events that had just passed. So numb that she threatened to walk. Said she needed a reason to keep going.

Dom gave her the only one he had. Her calm reaction to his being a rebel surprised him.

Her cut wasn't as bad as it had been for the girl he and Sheila had treated—the one the supervisors had taken to the infirmary. No, Anya was lucky in more ways than one.

Together, they left the horror of the third floor behind and moved to the fourth floor.

The new floor had its perks, but one negative: he and Anya had to be separated. The boys and girls dorm sat across from each other. One was a plain room with beds, the other was every boys' dream. A space with privacy screens—something the girls' dorm didn't have—and virtual reality headsets and liquor.

The participants surprised him. Not only had Warren made it, but Ash was still there. Given that he was supposed to be one floor ahead of Dom, he guessed he'd missed rotation. Dom recalled the conversation he'd overheard on the ground floor.

'The people in here are a means to an end.' That's what Ash had told Warren.

Someone showed him to his bed. That night he crashed, too tired to think. But the next day after dinner, he saw Ash standing at the window that offered a one-way view across the space. He had a bottle of beer in one hand and was watching the girls stumble back to their dorms, exhausted.

His first instinct was to tell Ash to dial down the creepy, but the loud, chatty boy from the ground floor was gone. In his place was someone with a raw, edgy desperation that made Dom steer clear.

Dom settled on his bed and cupped his hands behind his neck. He'd wanted more time in the prefab with Anya. Maybe she'd had time to think about his rebel status. Maybe she was planning ways to ruin his and Sheila's progress. It frustrated him to be separated from her right now.

But she'd accepted his story.

She was bleeding from a cut on her arm, desperate. She didn't have a choice but to accept your lies.

He shook his head to dislodge the feeling he got too often: that he would only hold her back. His games with Sheila had pulled her further into Arcis. And the only way to get out was to finish the game.

He touched his lips, remembering the feel of her there. Her soft mouth had been swollen from his raw need for her. When she'd pressed up against him, his body had reacted instantly. It was like she was made for him.

You're nothing but a liar, Dom Pavesi. You inherited that trait from your father. She's better off without you.

Sitting on the edge of the bed in the prefab, she'd stared up at him. Her pale skin made her dark-blue eyes pop. Then, when she'd kissed him... He'd imagined that for a long time. And it surpassed all expectations. It took his breath away. Literally. He hadn't trusted himself to stop.

Neither Kaylie nor Mia had stirred up a similar reaction in him. They'd been a distraction because his mother was missing and he'd killed his father. Their company had kept the darker thoughts at bay, but it never released him from it. What he felt for them was lust. A longing. A mutual convenience.

But Anya was different. His heart sounded like a runaway train whenever she was near. He could tell she had no experience, but he would never rush anything with her.

No. He would go at a pace she was comfortable with.

But when she'd pressed her body into his, teasing him with her tongue, breathing like she couldn't catch any air, he'd forgotten all about pacing. Because he'd felt the same way, as if the breath had been sucked out of him. Her skin was like cotton, soft and smooth. He'd tried to be good, but then his hands ended up where they did. She'd touched him, touched his skin.

God, Pavesi. Focus.

Found his scars...

That sent him crashing back to reality. She'd been looking for them. She'd already seen them in the bathroom. But he wasn't ready to talk about it, to admit his biggest weakness.

He sat up and craned his neck to look outside. Ash continued to drink at the window. Warren was sitting on one of the chairs and playing a battle through the VR headset.

Two people to keep a closer eye on.

A yawn caught him and he nodded off.

Ω

A whistle, loud and sharp, woke him.

'Gather round. Someone's here to *negotiate*.'

He roused from his sleep and got up. But the second he saw who it was, he froze. Anya stood in their dorm, her arms wrapped around her. She looked so vulnerable it ripped his heart in half. He wanted to drag her away, to keep her from whatever she was about to do—from whatever Ash had planned.

And where was Sheila? Why had she let Anya come here alone?

'What the hell are you doing here?'

She stiffened at his words.

Good. He wanted to frighten her, to make her understand it was a mistake coming here. He didn't trust Ash, and he hadn't figured out the purpose of the fourth floor yet. So far, Ash had been vague about it.

'She says she's here to do a deal,' said Ash.

Dom strode to the back of where the other boys had gathered, a surge of anger heating his skin. He folded his tense arms and concentrated on controlling his rapid breaths. He stared at Anya. She glanced at him, then blushed and focused on Ash.

Shit.

'We can't rotate off this floor *and* eat,' said Anya.

'It seems to be one choice or the other. We understand we will earn more points if we help you.'

Why can't you rotate and eat?

The boys hadn't been told how the girls earned points by themselves—only how the boys could earn points alone or with the girls' help. But he'd expected Sheila to hold out a little longer.

'We knew the girls would cave,' said Ash.

He touched Anya's hair. Dom growled, fresh anger flaring in his chest. He flexed his hands.

She jerked away from him. 'Don't touch me.'

Ash backed off, which was good, because if he touched her again he might kill him.

'Explain how we can help you,' said Anya. Her voice wobbled a little.

Turn around and leave. You don't want to know.

Ash led her over to the famous board, the one that listed all the activities.

He smirked at her. 'As you can see, we earn points for doing practically nothing. Of course, you're free to choose whatever you like. My personal favourite is the last one.' His fingers brushed across Anya's neck and she shivered.

Dom's anger rose again. His leg bounced. He dropped his hands to his side, ready to defend her.

Anya looked over suddenly, flashed him a warning look, then grabbed Ash's arm and twisted it behind his back. 'I haven't agreed to anything yet, so no touching. Okay?'

Ash sneered beneath her hold, but he couldn't break free. She was strong. Dom had felt that same strength when he'd taught her how to defend herself.

'Okay, okay. Being restrained by a beautiful girl is a turn-on, by the way.'

Dom relaxed his stance and looked at Anya again. She stood with her shoulders back and head held high. He didn't doubt she could take care of herself. But he didn't want her to. He wanted to protect her.

'Talk it over with the others if you must,' said Ash. 'But you'll be back.'

Ash watched Anya leave. Dom tensed up, waiting for him to say something smart. He moved closer to the window. Across the hall, he saw Sheila waiting for Anya in the entrance to their dorm. Anya said something to her; Sheila's eyes widened and she straightened up. The girls followed Anya into the bathroom.

No cameras. Good move.

Ash turned away from the window. Gone was the cocky smile and the brazen attitude. He chewed on his thumb, like the girls were his last hope. But it was the look of camaraderie he gave Warren that unsettled him the most.

Ω

The next day, Dom paced the large dorm as he waited for the girls to arrive with their answer. He'd spoken to Anya last night, reminded her to be careful. He had a proposal for her, something he'd agreed with Jerome. But she'd hit him with a plan of her own. One that involved Warren and rotation. She'd told him he and Sheila needed to rotate without her.

Sane and sensible Dom saw merit in her idea. Unpredictable Dom, who over thought everything, hated the plan.

It was a terrible idea. He needed to keep her safe. After all, he'd encouraged Anya to venture deeper into his hellhole.

But she was right. Damn it.

He and Sheila had a job to do.

But pairing up with Warren Hunt? No way. He didn't trust him, and he would find a way to scupper his progress.

With Frank gone, Jerome was the natural fit for her. His response had surprised him.

'No way. Frank died because of her. I can't forgive her.'

'Jerome, you got it all wrong. Frank tried to open the door. She almost died trying to save him.'

Dom snapped out of his thoughts when Ash started towards the door and opened it.

'Welcome to *mi casa*, ladies.'

One by one, the girls entered the room. Dom's gaze found Anya. She held herself more confidently than the day before. Sheila, on the other hand, looked terrified. June stood close to her, observing her surroundings with a neutral eye—the way all rebel soldiers had been trained to do.

Ash gestured for the girls to sit.

'Okay, let's see who gets to choose one of these lovely ladies first.'

Not for the first time, Ash's cockiness and bravado slipped, enough for Dom to notice his desperation. He didn't give off the same uneasy vibe as Warren. But it didn't make him any less dangerous.

The only conclusion he came to was that Ash was as nervous as the girls.

The boys picked the girls. Dom would choose last. His act of kindness in securing food for the girls had carried a hefty penalty.

Ash chose Lilly. A quiet, timid girl. Someone who would guarantee rotation.

'Don't worry, Lilly,' said Ash to her. 'We'll start out with something... easy.'

He bit his tongue, remembering Ash's words to Warren on the ground floor: 'Find someone who will get you rotated faster.'

Jerome was up next and he chose Anya, like they'd agreed. Dom gave him a discreet nod. Warren didn't look happy about it. That wasn't Dom's problem.

Warren ended up with June. He knew Shaw could handle herself, but he wanted to speak to her soon before they got separated again, to find out what she'd learned about Tahlia. He'd also ask her to scupper Warren's chances of rotating. He wasn't sure why, but his gut warned him he could be a problem for him and Sheila.

Sheila was left and Dom picked her.

She came to his side, her eyes downcast. She mouthed *sorry* at him.

It suddenly became clear to him why Anya had come to the dorm the day before instead of Sheila. He cupped her neck and brought his lips close to her ear. 'We'll find a way to do this without actually doing anything. Okay?'

She nodded timidly, and he wanted to pull her into a tight hug. But he caught Anya watching before she turned away, looking embarrassed. Jerome tapped her on the shoulder and the pair moved to a quieter part of the room.

'I'm sorry, Dom. Anya volunteered to come here yesterday. I tried, but I couldn't be here. Not with this lot.'

'It's okay, Sheila. I talked to her last night. I arranged for Jerome to pick her. It's all going to work out fine.'

Sheila smirked. 'She's got balls. That girl might actually be growing on me.'

'Hands off. I saw her first.'

Sheila folded her arms and looked around nervously. 'So what do we do now?' Other couples stood around the activity board discussing the options.

Dom pulled her into his sectioned-off bedroom with enough standing room for two people. His hoodie from the third floor lay on the ground. He gestured for her to sit on his bed and sat beside her.

'Nothing you don't want to do. We can work up the points safely or we can go straight to the top, and do the thing that earns us the most points.'

Sheila bit her lip, shook her head. 'I can't have sex with you. I'm sorry.'

He leaned in close. 'I don't mean literally. I got to thinking: how does Arcis know what we're doing and when?'

Sheila looked at him as if he'd lost his mind. 'The cameras, Dom?'

He spoke in a hushed voice. 'And you think you'd be okay having sex on camera?'

Sheila shuddered. 'Okay, then what?'

'What if you decided to do it off camera, like in one of the bathrooms, for privacy, where there are no cameras? How would anyone know?'

Sheila shrugged.

Dom held out his wrist and tapped the spot with his chip. 'Proximity,' he said. 'It has to count for something. The chip stores data. Why not transmit data too? What if it detects elevated heart rates? It's positioned over a pulse spot.'

'So, we work up our heart rates, get close and that's it?'

'I don't know, but it's a theory I'd like to try.'

Sheila smiled. 'Well, if it means skipping the hot and sweaty with you, then I'm all for it.'

Dom touched his heart. 'Thanks, Sheila. That really gives my ego a boost.'

'Your ego doesn't need it.'

He switched the subject. 'So what's going on with you and Yasmin?' He'd noticed a connection between Sheila and a girl who'd rotated from the second floor.

Sheila shifted to look at him. 'What do you mean?'

'You two seem close.'

She shrugged. 'I barely know her. She's nice. But I'm not sure she's my type, to be honest.'

Yasmin was a good distraction for Sheila. Not the right fit, though. Yasmin was too tough, too closed off for her.

Sheila sighed as she stood up. 'Come on, Dom Juan. Let's get this over with.'

16

'You can't save everybody,' said Sheila.

She stood beside Dom on the fifth-floor walkway. Their efforts to fool the controllers into thinking they had sex had paid off. But Lilly had just jumped over the side after blasting Ash with electricity and watching him fall to his death.

Ash had forced himself on Lilly.

It sickened him to think both of them could be alive if he'd shared his theory with them.

But three hours into the morning, rotation had been called. Their decision to rotate almost everyone made no sense, given the haphazard scores.

Anya had made it, but so had Warren. A nasty bruise marked his jaw line.

He watched her as she looked over the side, looking down to where Lilly and Ash had landed. Her face was wiped clean of emotion, as though she'd seen too much already. But she couldn't mask the pain in her eyes. She was covering her injured arm with her hand. He'd seen it moments ago; the wound looked like it had been reopened.

She straightened up and clutched her Electro Gun tight to her body. In the room next to the changing room was a station with Electro Guns. It was how Lilly had been able to attack Ash.

She watched the walkway as she crossed to the second Tower.

Something had happened to her. And now she was ignoring him.

'What's going on with Anya?' Dom asked Sheila as they crossed. 'Her wound, it looks fresh. Did something happen?'

Sheila shrugged. 'Hell if I know. That girl's a walking disaster.'

Dom held his gun close to his chest and followed Sheila into Tower B, unconvinced by her explanation.

In front of them was a maze, laid out differently to the one on the third. The fifth floor room was twice as big, and this maze appeared to have multiple entry points. The other difference was they had guns, and Dom couldn't spot any gold doors.

The male supervisor explained the purpose of the new floor. Dom tagged on to the game at the console by the door and raced for one of the entrances.

Deafening music drowned out his senses, leaving little room to think. He pushed past the noise designed to disorientate him, concentrating instead on the combat and strategy elements to the task ahead. The male supervisor had warned them the maze would change as soon as they learned a route. Dom followed the corridors as fast as he could, firing at black discs that counted as scores. Then the time ran out, and the absence of music left behind a loud ringing in his ears. The walls lowered into the floor. The supervisor waited by the scoreboard positioned to the rear of the maze.

'Dom won that round,' he said. 'He found six of the discs in the time allowed. But Anya tried something different. Why don't you tell everyone what you did?'

Dom frowned.

Anya stood straight, gripping the Electro Gun in both hands and pressing it to her chest. She knew how to use a gun. That much was obvious.

'I shot at the wall. It's organic and I was able to pass through.'

'But you wound up trapped?'

She nodded.

'Anya cheated and the maze trapped her,' said the supervisor. 'When she ran out of charge she could no longer progress. How many discs did you find?'

'Four.'

'The lesson is clear. You can cheat and guarantee a low score, or you can play it fair and find more discs. The latter will take you longer but it is achievable.'

The supervisor dismissed them for the night and the girls made a beeline for the dining hall. He didn't blame them, not after their near starvation on the floor below. Dom leaned against the wall outside, waiting for them to finish. He couldn't put off his chat with June any longer. Any new information might give them an edge over the controllers in Arcis.

Twenty minutes later, the girls emerged. Anya caught his eye briefly before marching on to the dormitory.

His gut twisted. What had he done wrong? He pushed aside his confusion to catch up with June.

'Hey, can I have a quick word?'

June fell to the back of the group and nodded towards the bathroom. They entered and June dropped the pretence to give him a long hug.

She pulled back and smiled at him. 'Dom, I've been dying to catch up with you.'

'Me, too. Is everything going okay for you?'

She nodded. 'Nothing I can't handle.'

'And Warren? What happened on the floor below?'

She ran her hand through her fine-blonde hair and exhaled. 'I did everything I could to stop him from progressing, but this place seems to change the rules whenever it likes. I'm not sure it's possible to keep him away. If Arcis wants him to progress, it'll happen.'

'Thanks for trying, anyway.' Dom paused. 'I get a funny vibe off him.'

'Yeah, me too.'

'Everything happened so fast, I haven't had a chance to ask you about Tahlia,' said Dom. 'I'm sorry about what happened to her. What did you find out?'

'Well, her parents worked in Praesidium. Her mother was hired as an artist, her father as a gardener. They worked there for a while. Tahlia even lived in the city when she was younger.'

'Did she remember much about it?'

'Not much. She was young. She described the place as bright, white and sterile. Her family lived in an apartment complex in one of the five zones in the city. She mentioned Praesidium had a really good art programme. She mostly travelled between her apartment and the school there. But Tahlia also assumed a lot about the city, so I don't think she was allowed to see much of the place. She mentioned that whenever she tried to explore, someone would accompany her. One of the women, from the apartment block where she lived, stayed with her when her parents were working.'

Dom leaned against the sink and rubbed his jaw. 'I think Arcis targeted Tahlia on the first floor. They singled her out for a reason.'

June nodded. 'I believe that, too. Anya was tricked

into helping keep her in last place. She felt terrible about it. Warren had a hand in that.'

Dom stiffened. 'Did he? How?'

'Yasmin told me he'd overheard the male and female supervisor say they'd rotate everyone if someone was consistently last A few of them discussed it and agreed Tahlia should be left behind because she was the slowest.'

Dom frowned. 'It's possible he wasn't lying about that. I heard the same thing. My group targeted someone, a girl called Brianna. I think we were set up. I'd love to know if Brianna had been to Praesidium before, and if she'd ever lived there.'

'So you think Arcis knew about Tahlia? That they recognised her from the city?'

'Or she's in the system. Did she say why her parents left Praesidium and returned to the towns?'

June shrugged. 'Only that they didn't think it was the right place to bring up a child.'

'So her parents are murdered and Tahlia is taken to Arcis. They run her through a couple of floors before they kill her.'

June nodded and stuffed her hands into her pockets. 'Maybe Arcis wanted to know what she remembered about the city. Maybe she talked too much about it. Compliance doesn't affect memory. It's possible the controllers chose to kill her before she could talk about anything else.'

Dom ran a hand down his face. '*Jesus.*' After a moment, he looked at June. 'Hey, what's going on with Anya? She seems off.'

June concentrated on the sink. 'You should ask her. It's not my place.'

His heart battered against his ribcage. 'What does *that* mean?'

June looked up at him. 'It means you have to ask her, Dom. Sorry.'

Dom forced a smile. 'Okay, and I'm glad you're with us.'

She hugged him again. 'Me, too. We'll get there, Dom. You've lost someone. So have I. We'll get answers if it's the last thing we do.'

He hoped so, because so far nothing was making much sense. They headed to the dorm separately. Dom entered after June, walking in on an argument between Sheila and Anya over who got the bed closer to the door. June pulled Sheila away to another bed and whispered something to her. Sheila glanced at Anya and nodded.

What the hell?

He watched Anya as he walked past her. She was sitting on the first bed with her knees pulled up tight to her chest, and was resting a cheek on her knees. Jerome had taken the bed next to hers.

Maybe it had something to do with Jerome. They hadn't talked properly, that's all. But it didn't explain the cut on her arm, its seam beaded with fresh dried blood.

Dom took the bed opposite hers. Despite their proximity, it felt like she was a million miles away. He wanted to help her through her grief. But only Jerome could take away her guilt.

'I decided something today,' said Jerome.

June looked up. 'What?'

'I'm going to finish this programme. I'm going to do it for Frank. It's what he would have done for me.'

Dom looked away. He didn't know Frank and it felt too intimate a moment to be a part of.

'We all finish for Frank and Tahlia,' said June.

Anya added, 'And Lilly.'

Dom looked back. She was sitting up straight, her

legs on the floor. His chest warmed to see her more alert, but something still wasn't right. He could see it in her eyes.

Two boys who'd rotated from the third floor discussed the gold door. As soon as they did, Anya's newfound confidence melted away. He curled his hands into the duvet. The uneasy moment passed.

He stared at her, looked away, stared at his hands. What should he do? He glanced at her again, but her gaze was so sad he couldn't bear to see it.

'So, how did you know to shoot the wall?' said Jerome.

This caught Dom's attention. How had Anya figured it out?

'Uh?'

'The wall. You said it was organic.'

Anya shrugged. 'I put my hand on it and it didn't feel like a real wall. I was getting turned around so much it felt like the maze was closing me in.'

'And it did, eventually,' said Jerome.

'Yeah. Wasn't a smart tactic.'

They talked about strategy for the next game. Dom used the discussion as an excuse to move closer to Anya.

'Dom,' said Sheila, 'you should partner with Anya and June.'

He caught the angry look Anya gave Sheila.

Being on the outside irritated him, but he shook his errant thoughts about Anya away. They'd reached the fifth floor; that was over the half way point. Dom needed to remember his and Sheila's goal to reach the ninth floor.

The lights dimmed before they went out for the night—a sign that the force field was down.

While everyone was occupied, he flicked the raised area behind one ear, activating the communication card that allowed him to communicate with Preston, Max and Charlie. He sent a message.

We're on the fifth floor. You were right. Tahlia Odare was targeted.

Hold on. We're working on getting— The reply cut off.

Hurry, he tapped out, not sure if the message made it through.

The deeper Dom ventured into Arcis, the shorter the time to communicate with the outside became.

He flexed his hands as a new worry took hold.

17

Dom and the others had spent less than a day on the fifth floor. In fact, rotation happened just after the second round in the combat maze. Arcis was rushing them through the floors. Just nine of them had made it.

The lights flickered overhead. It was Anya who had noticed the vibrations that happened just before rotation. Something big must be causing both events. Dom passed on new details to Preston, the communications operative located outside Essention. He'd managed to fire a bunch of short messages back, but the communication didn't last long.

When Anya relayed her feelings to him about the supervisors, Dom listened. She'd said that at first glance, there seemed to be just two supervisors, a male and a female, but variances in their appearance from floor to floor hinted that there might be more of them.

He should have noticed the vibrations, but his business with Ash and Warren had distracted him from the truth. Anya saw things he didn't, and in this place it could be the difference between life and death.

Ash may not have survived, but Warren was still a threat.

Her aggressive strategy in the maze had surprised him. But what shocked him was when she'd pumped a few rounds of nonlethal electricity into Warren's body. Something had happened between them and Dom hadn't noticed. What happened with Brianna had shaken his confidence, made him second guess the feeling in his gut. And it was now telling him Warren was a danger.

He became attuned to Anya's varying moods. Sometimes she was up, others down. Their arrival on the seventh floor—skipping the sixth entirely—didn't ease her anxiety much. Three others—two boys and a girl from the sixth floor—joined them shortly after. Anya's group and Jerome's group, plus Yasmin, Sheila and Warren had made it.

Maybe it was Warren's presence that made her brow crease with worry, or had her biting her lip. Dom hated not knowing how to fix things for her.

The female supervisor showed up and took them to Tower B, past a bunch of upright white leather seats that looked like examination chairs. Each had a raised footrest and a monitor attached to the side. While the supervisor spoke, Dom watched for the differences Anya had mentioned. They were subtle—a slightly thinner face or different hairstyle—and not something he would have noticed on his own.

The supervisor left them alone in the dining hall. Dom stood by the food counter while Anya sat quietly at the table. Warren was talking to the other boys. He watched him for a while, his eyes flicking between an animated Warren and a despondent Anya.

Sheila joined him and pulled him away to a corner of the room.

'What's gotten into you?' she hissed.

'I can't stand this, Sheila. I feel like I'm losing

control in here.' He ran his hands through his soft curly hair. It had been at least six weeks since Charlie had buzz-cut it.

'Well, pull yourself together. You can't fall apart on me, you hear?'

He turned back to the room. His eyes cut to Anya who had just stood up and was walking to the door, backpack in hand. He tracked her all the way out. Warren didn't react to her leaving.

When she was gone, he faced Sheila and whispered, 'Okay, spill. I want to know what you know.'

Sheila pressed a hand to her heart. 'I know nothing more than you do. I swear.'

'What's going on with Anya? And don't tell me it's nothing. I'm not stupid. She's acting weird and you and Yasmin know something.'

Sheila bit her lip; a tell-tale sign she was hiding something.

'Sheila...'

'I promised not to say anything.'

He gripped the sides of her arms. 'Tell me.'

Sheila pulled in a long breath and released it. 'It's about Anya.'

'Yeah, I figured. What about her?'

Sheila leaned in closer. 'Promise you won't freak out, especially not in here?'

Dom looked back at the others. They were all engaged in conversation. June flashed Sheila a warning look.

So June knows, too?

He ignored her and concentrated on Sheila. 'Out with it.'

'Promise me you won't overreact.'

Dom nodded.

'I mean it. Promise, Dom. Out loud.'

He sighed. 'I promise.'

'It's Warren.'

His rate of pulse multiplied by twelve. 'What about him?'

Sheila whispered. 'He forced himself on Anya last night.'

'*What?*'

Sheila shushed him. 'You didn't notice the nasty bruise on his jaw and cheek? That was the little Spitfire giving him what he deserved.'

Dom glared at Warren. He sat stiffer than usual, not looking at anyone in particular. June got to her feet and walked out of the room.

He stared at Sheila. 'She did that? She hit him?' His heart refused to settle.

Sheila smirked. 'Turns out she has a mean right hook. June found her first.'

'I need to talk to her, see if she's okay.'

He turned to go, but Sheila grabbed his arm. 'No. Not unless she says she wants to speak to you. She's been through something traumatic. She needs time to deal.'

Dom stared at her hand on his. 'I won't upset her. And why wouldn't she want to speak to me?'

She let go. 'She needs her space, and that means from you.'

He sighed as he realised. 'She's avoiding me.'

'Look, sometimes girls just need the company of other girls. Okay?'

It wasn't okay and he didn't care. 'I need to see her. And you're going to make that happen.'

'You think I'm your private love guru or something?' He lifted a brow at her and Sheila huffed out a breath. 'Fine. What do you want me to do?'

'Tell her I want to see her. Tell her now.'

'No can do.'

'Fine. Then I'll go myself.'

She shook his arm. 'Do that and Anya will not only be pissed off with me, but she'll probably throw you out.'

'I can't control much in here but if I can help her, I want to try.'

Sheila slumped against the wall, as if defeated. 'I don't want to get in the middle of this.'

'You're already in the middle. You put yourself there when you kept a secret, a big one, from me. Did you really think I wouldn't find out about it? I've been warning you about that weirdo for a while now.'

'And I didn't see it. I'm sorry. But you should know Anya doesn't want to mess up our chances to rotate.'

The fight drained out of Dom. He dropped his gaze to the floor. 'Yeah, she told me the same thing.' He looked up. 'I just didn't think she'd put her life in danger to do it.'

'Look,' said Sheila. 'I can see you care for her, but you have to play it cool. Eyes are watching. You don't always have to be in control, you know.'

Control was all he had left. 'Tell her I want to see her now and I'll stop bugging you about it.'

Sheila levelled a glare at him; it was a look that would have most men quivering at her feet. He stared back, waiting for the tiny flicker of change in her expression.

There it is.

'*Fine.* But you wait until I ask her. If she says no, you leave it alone. Got it?'

Dom nodded.

His heart thumped as he walked past Warren to the exit. He kept his eyes forward, because if he looked at him, he might finish the job on his face that Anya had started. Sheila slipped into the dorm room while he waited outside.

He bit his thumbnail. His back dripped with sweat. His racing pulse drowned out any clarity of thought. What if she said no? Could he be around Warren without beating him to a pulp?

June slipped out of the dorm room and gave him a pat on the arm as she passed.

Then Sheila came out. 'All yours. And behave.'

His shaking legs carried him inside the room. Anya was sitting on the bed with her arms wrapped around her legs. He wanted to go to her, to console her. But he didn't want to frighten her and give her another reason to shut him out.

He stood by the door, hands in his pockets, fingers playing the keys on his old piano at home. Counting helped to calm him.

'I thought you'd like to know,' said Dom. 'I passed on your theory.' He was referring to the information about the vibrations between the floors. He'd also told Preston that he suspected his cover—and also Sheila's and June's cover—had been blown.

'Good.'

Dom looked down, his chest tight with anger. 'Sheila told me what happened with Warren.'

'She shouldn't have done that,' she snapped. Her anger surprised him. 'So I guess everyone knows?'

He slipped his hands out of his pockets. They were already fists. He ground them into the sides of his legs. Her secrets were safe with him, she had to know that. Sheila had barely told him anything.

Dom moved into the room. 'Not everyone.'

Without her, he felt lost at sea, set adrift in past memories. She anchored him in the present.

He sat down on her bed. 'Why didn't you tell me?'

'What would you have done if I had?'

'Knocked Warren out, probably.'

That coaxed a smile out of her. 'I already did that. I didn't need you coming to my rescue.'

Dom grinned. 'I know, I saw.' But it also burned him up that June had been the one to rescue her, not him. His smile slipped away. 'I can't sit back and watch bad things happen to you. Don't you get that yet?'

She bit her lip. 'You and Sheila need to reach the ninth floor. I can't be a distraction.'

'If you hadn't noticed, we're doing just fine.'

Anya stiffened and lowered her eyes. 'I had. I saw your scores on the fourth floor.'

He'd meant it to reassure her. It never occurred to him that she might misunderstand how he and Sheila had obtained their scores.

Smooth, Pavesi. Get yourself out of this mess.

She stiffened when he scooted closer to her. 'You think Sheila and I were... together.'

Anya pulled her legs in tighter, creating a physical barrier between them. 'It's none of my business, Dom. Really.'

She blushed and he started to laugh. He couldn't help it—it just came out.

'Here, let me show you what we did.'

Anya looked at him, startled. 'I don't think we need to—'

This needed action, not words. He pressed their chips together and told her his theory about proximity. He still had a grip on her wrist when she stared up at him. The memory of their night in the first-aid prefab came back to him, right before they'd kissed. Now he wanted to taste her again.

But images of what Warren had done flashed through his mind and made it hard to relax. He rotated her injured arm gently.

'Is this still bothering you?' His voice burned with anger.

'No. It's beginning to heal.'

Her voice, soft and gentle, dissolved some of his rage. A new fire surged through his veins. His gaze drifted from her mouth to her eyes.

Anya looked down at his hand on her arm. 'I don't think *this* counts as a score on this floor.'

Then tell me to stop touching you.

He grabbed her legs and pulled her towards him. Her eyes widened a fraction, but she didn't protest. When he touched her face, she shivered.

You're an insensitive ass, Pavesi.

He pulled back. 'I'm sorry. I shouldn't have presumed—'

Anya drew his hands back to her face. 'No, it's fine. I just... It's nothing.'

He imagined himself on the range, firing off a hundred shots into a target with a picture of Warren's face on it. It took some effort to remember to breathe.

Anya's bright, trusting eyes, marred with dark secrets, stared up at him. He made a better effort to keep his anger under control.

'You're so beautiful, Anya. In more ways than you know.'

She shook her head. 'Sheila is beautiful. I'm ordinary.'

He almost laughed. Sure, Sheila had the right genetics. But Dom preferred uniqueness over perfection, and he told her so.

Anya grinned. 'I'd like to be taller.'

'What's wrong with the height you are?'

'The tall girls usually get the boys.'

'Is that so?'

'Sheila always turns heads.'

'Well, she doesn't turn mine. I prefer girls around five feet six with cinnamon-brown hair, beautifully pale skin and dark-blue eyes that I could stare at all day. If you know anyone who fits that description, would you give me a heads-up?'

Anya pushed him playfully and smiled before inching closer.

Dom froze. He didn't want to scare her, but he needed to feel her.

He drew her face to his and placed a light kiss on her mouth, if only to reassure her that he was the opposite of Warren. But when she leaned into him without warning, he lost all self control. Without asking, he pulled her onto his lap in one swift movement. Her legs slid either side of him, shortening his breaths.

'Is this okay?' he asked. 'I just wanted to feel you again.'

She responded by wrapping her arms around him. He started slow, his kiss feather-light and gentle. Her touch left trails of fire along his arm, on his neck. His own hands quivered from keeping a tight lid on his feelings. But then she shifted in his lap and the fire inside him burned hotter.

Dom parted her lips with a new urgency. He needed to taste her, to experience her more intimately than before. Anya arched into him, pressing her lips to his. Her tongue swept along his bottom lip, drawing a groan from him. She fit her body against him in a way that made him think she wanted more. He looked up at her, wanting it, too—God, how he wanted it—but not here, not where cameras and operators watched their intimate moment. The thought sickened him.

Anya must have sensed the same thing because she pulled back from him. He groaned as her lack of body heat left him feeling cold inside.

She stayed sitting on his legs and cupped his face. 'You're perfect.'

Dom didn't agree. 'I'm not.' His eyes dropped to her throat. 'Not like you.'

His scars, the ones he was terrified to show her, proved that. Every time he got undressed, they served as a reminder that he was only half a man. The other scars, the emotional ones his father had carved into him, cut deeper and made him doubt himself every day.

He watched, curious, as she moved to sit behind him.

She placed her hands on the outside of his T-shirt.

No. No!

She tugged up the edges.

He grabbed her hands. 'Anya. What are you—'

'Please, let me see.'

'No.'

'Why?'

'Please, Anya. I—'

Don't ask me to show you. I hate them and what they represent. A lost childhood, a lifetime of compensating for my physical loss. I'm not who you think I am. I'm a killer. I murdered my father and I can barely control my anger most days. I thank Carlo for that.

He kept a tight grip on her hands. She didn't say anything, didn't move away. Sheila had seen the scars by accident. Kaylie had seen them when they'd fooled around and taken things further in a darkened room. So had Mia. The look of shock on their faces told him enough.

Maybe Anya was different from Mia and Kaylie. He wanted to believe it.

But he couldn't bear to see the same shock or disgust when she saw how ugly his body looked naked.

He loosened his grip on her hand and leaned forward. She pulled the fabric up without hesitation.

Dom waited for the gasp, similar to how she'd reacted in the bathroom when he'd spilled hot coffee on himself. He'd known that would be her reaction. It was everyone's reaction at first. But all he heard was a quiet, steady breath. And when Anya traced his C-shaped scar that ran from under his armpit to the middle of his back, he jerked.

Anya pulled away, but touched her warm fingers to his skin.

'Does it hurt?' she whispered.

'The opposite,' said Dom. He turned partially. 'I just don't like people seeing it.'

'Sheila says you have more.'

He undid his belt buckle, unbuttoned his combats and inched the waistband down a little.

Anya ran her finger along the straight scar running from the middle of his back, curving around his left side. He shivered beneath her touch.

'And another one on the front.' He turned around to face her, so she could see the straight line across his flat abdomen with a small intersecting cut in the centre, heading north.

'What happened?'

He explained his sickness, his surgeries. She asked about Sheila. He told her how they knew each other.

Anya fell silent.

'I wanted to show you before now,' said Dom, his voice tight with emotion, 'but I didn't know how you'd react. It's not attractive.'

She bent her head and kissed him, along his scars. The feel of her there both terrified and soothed him.

'Like I said, perfect.'

She looped her arms around him and pressed her cheek to his back. For the first time in years, his scars didn't control him. Anya's touch had soothed his anger over what they'd stolen from him.

Her gentle, assured touch passed new strength to him. The longer they sat there, the more he knew he had to find a way to live with his weakness.

Sheila appeared at the door and they pulled apart. But the separation didn't bother him. He would find a way to protect her, to protect his friends and get them out of this place.

18

The last seven floors had been a breeze compared to the eighth. During that time he'd come to accept his scars and learn that not everything was within his control. Then the worst thing happened that undid all his good work.

Dom ran a shaky hand across his neck. 'What are they doing? I mean, how?'

Anya stood beside him in the eighth-floor room, on one side of a large, red velvet curtain. Five of them, including Sheila June and Yasmin, had rotated from the seventh floor a couple of hours ago after answering questions designed to test their loyalty. Warren had been forced to repeat the seventh floor, so that was one small mercy. Anya had received a message from her brother, Jason: the rebels were inside Arcis and were coming for them. A final question of who to save, Sheila or Anya, had shaken Dom to the core.

But the shame of picking someone did not compare to how he felt now. On the other side of the curtain, Sheila, June and Yasmin looked after babies ranging in ages. A frosted-glass wall and a curtain shielded the nightmare from them.

He stared at the large Perspex box before him,

divided down into sections and each one containing a child. But it was the sight of a boy clutching the stubby crayon that escalated his worst fears. When the boy leaned forward over his picture and Dom saw his perfect C-shaped scar, he almost threw up.

He swallowed back bile just as Anya finished her full circle of the box. She was looking for a way inside. Dom couldn't tear his gaze from the boy, no older than four, who ignored them while they stood there and watched him colour.

A girl around the same age as the boy stretched and flashed a scar on her waist similar to his own.

He drew in a tight breath and tugged on his hair. 'What are they doing here?' He felt Anya's eyes on him. 'Why does he have—?'

Anya pinned his arms down by his side. The move was meant to calm him but it had the opposite effect. Rage, confusion and terror made him want to run. Why were these scarred children here? Where were their parents?

The more he watched the children, the more unsettled he became by their quiet natures. They lacked the energy of normal kids.

'Maybe they were sick, like you were,' said Anya.

He didn't answer her, because it was the only explanation. Were these children part of Praesidium's programme, too?

He'd been so focused on the scars and the embarrassment of having them that it never occurred to him his surgeries might have been planned. That his father had made a deal with the doctors in Praesidium to use Dom as some sort of lab rat.

He almost laughed because it made sense now. Carlo would disappear for a month after each surgery and return a sober, attentive father for about a week. He'd never questioned where Carlo had gone, but Dom suspected payment for his surgeries may have funded his bender. He could picture Carlo now: drunk off his ass for a month, then reaching that tipping point where he couldn't stand the sight of alcohol.

'Talk to me!' Anya yelled at him.

Dom snapped his gaze back to her. He grabbed her hand and pulled her back to the babies on the other side of the curtain.

'I don't know. I just don't... I need to leave.'

He felt his knees go weak. Anya supported his weight with an arm around his middle. He leaned into her for a moment then righted himself. Now was not the time to lose his focus. That's what Arcis wanted. If he was to survive this place, if he was to find his mother, he had to stay strong. He had no proof but Dom knew his father, and selling him to science was something he would do. And if he really thought about it, Carlo had been too interested in Dom's hospital visits for there not to be something in it for him.

The lights dipped suddenly; a strong vibration in the floor followed. For the first time, Dom didn't report either event to Preston.

He busied himself with the babies while Anya watched him from a safe distance outside the box. He'd lived his life being the strong one, being the shoulder for everyone else to lean on. But inside, he barely kept things together. One look at Anya and he'd lose it for sure.

One of the boy babies made a laughing sound and he picked him up, checking his eyes, checking for hidden scars, searching for signs of a life that mirrored his own. To his relief, the baby had no scars and looked normal, right down to the pigmentation in his eyes.

Not like the children in the next room.

An hour later, the female supervisor appeared.

'Put the babies down. We've learned all we can from your interactions. You're being rotated to the final floor.'

Dom returned the baby to his crib and tucked a blanket around his wriggling body. The baby kicked it off and cried at Dom's absence. He left the box and the crying babies behind and followed the supervisor to the elevator.

Only one more floor remained: the heart of Arcis and the source of the power dips and vibrations. This close to freedom, Dom didn't know if they would make it out alive.

19

The giant machine in the centre of the room rattled, sending deep vibrations through Dom's legs.

Mariella wasn't here. Neither was June's sister.

The same hidden voice that had greeted them upon their arrival on the ninth floor, spoke once more.

It was pushing them to enter the machine. Anya had called the voice Quintus. Where and when had she heard that name?

Quintus knew Dom, knew his mother. It only confirmed the truth: Dom had been experimented upon, possibly made sick by the city, or by his own father, so the surgeries would look more natural.

Anya's distraction of Quintus had stopped working. She'd been stalling so Max and her brother had time to get here. And they did. Preston was with him. Then the shooting started. Two soldiers and Preston dropped to the ground.

A shocked Anya volunteered to go through the machine. He'd tried to take her place but Quintus wouldn't take the bait.

If Anya was scared, she hid it well. He, on the other hand, wanted to demand why the city had used him, and to ask where his mother—and June's sister—were.

But the threats to Anya's brother, Max and the remaining soldier silenced him.

Anya walked through the first part of the machine after the supervisors shot the soldiers. In the second part, a blue light scanned her from head to toe. She paused in front of a mirror in the third part and stared at a reflection of herself.

'Don't forget!' Dom yelled. Anya didn't turn around. She continued to look at her reflection, like she wasn't really there.

Quintus warned they'd lose their memories of this place. Dom's memories of Sheila and June would be safe, because they had met before. But everything in Arcis, every piece of knowledge he'd learned, every experience he'd had, would be stripped from him and probably passed on to Praesidium. Including his suspicions about his surgeries.

Anya walked through the mirror and disappeared. *Where did she go?* He stared at what he now realised was a portal.

His heart slammed against his ribcage. 'Where did you send her? Tell me!' He yelled at the voices until Sheila grabbed hold of his arm.

'We're going to the same place,' she whispered. 'You'll see her again. You need to calm the hell down.'

He bit his bottom lip so hard he tasted blood. Something moved in the mirror—or the portal. He yanked his arm out of Sheila's grip and moved closer. A residual image appeared to be stuck there. But when the image became whole and moved from the back of the portal to stand in front of it, Dom jerked back from it.

A dazed and naked Anya stared into the portal.

'Anya!' Dom shouted, averting his eyes. He ignored

Sheila's new warnings to keep quiet.

This odd version of Anya never turned around. She stepped through the portal.

When it was gone, Sheila said, 'What the hell was that?'

'That was a copy,' said the voice. 'A perfect replica of her. Hurry. We don't have much time. You all must step through the machine to complete the process.'

'And if we don't?' said Dom.

'Then I will order these men's deaths.'

Dom's gaze flickered over to where Max, his commanding officer, and Jason and the third soldier were being restrained by the almost identical male supervisors. Copies, he now realised. Anya had been right when she'd said that on each floor the supervisors were a little different.

Sheila stepped towards the machine. He didn't stop her. He wanted to go last, to make sure Max, Jason and the remaining soldier were okay. Sheila took the same route as Anya. When she passed through the first part of the arch, he saw her go from alert to despondent in a matter of seconds.

The first part must erase memories.

When it came to his turn, he would fight the process.

Sheila passed under the blue scanner and stepped through the portal. Dom shuddered when her naked copy did the same thing one minute later.

It was June's turn next, then Yasmin's.

Dom stepped forward last. He glanced at the rebels. 'Max, I'll come find you.'

Jason squirmed against the supervisor restraining him. 'Anya's all the family I have left. Keep her safe.'

He nodded. With every ounce of strength, he would

return to Anya. And if all traces of her were erased from his mind, he would find a way to keep the memory of her alive.

Dom scaled the short steps, stared up at the arch and shielded his eyes from the bright white lights. His memories thinned out, became wispy. He reached out for them, but it felt like they no longer belonged to him. The last thing he remembered was his conversation with Jason. But even that lacked certainty.

The machine pulled him, almost magnetically, under the blue scanner to stand in front of the portal. Activity began in the space behind it. He watched as the lower part of a torso materialised in front of him. It began with two feet, then two legs, then it stopped just below the start of the hipbone.

'Why has the replication process stopped?' commanded the voice.

Another voice, quiet until now, replied, 'The machine can only copy biological parts, Quintus. He has Praesidium tech in him.'

'What do you mean "Praesidium tech"?' said Dom, staring at what he assumed was a replica of his legs.

'He must be one of the earlier subjects, Quintus,' said the voice. 'We assumed he did not survive, like the others.'

'Erase this moment from his memory. We must study him further. I want to know how he has survived for so long with our tech.'

The machine whirred around him and Dom became dizzy and light-headed. Then the mirror pulled him forward.

20

A man dressed in white spoke to another in similar clothing. 'He's to be taken to the harvesting centre.' They stood by the entrance to an all-white room that Dom and the others had woken up in an hour ago.

'What about the others?' said the second man.

'They've been already assigned. The Collective wants this one to be taken for further study.'

Dom vaguely recalled a similar conversation: two voices arguing over him, one telling the other something hadn't worked right. The girl called Anya had already been taken away by a dark-skinned woman in a vibrant green dress. He heard them mention something about a library.

Sheila, June and a wiry blonde-haired girl were taken from the room, leaving Dom alone and barefoot. He glanced down at his outfit of white trousers and white top. He was dressed identically to the men who had come to take him.

'Who are you?' he said. 'Is this Praesidium?'

The men talked about him as if he wasn't there. Snippets of unfamiliar memories slipped back into place. He had stepped into some kind of machine. The lights had dazzled him. That happened moments before he'd come to this empty room.

Dom had made a promise to a man he hadn't met before, to keep someone safe. Max was there, and a soldier he didn't know. He couldn't remember why they'd stood together in a large space with a machine in the centre. Or why he'd been staring at a half-completed torso.

With a shake of his head, he tuned in to the conversation between the two men by the open door.

'The procedure didn't work. The copy didn't take. He is to be enrolled in the harvesting programme.'

'Why this one?'

'Quintus says he is part of a testing group from twelve years ago. The Collective lost track of them when their tracers stopped working. They were all presumed not to have survived. The Collective wishes to learn from him now.'

'Will we also be given the opportunity to learn?' said the other man.

'If the Collective wishes. Hurry. We must move him. I feel Quintus in my head. He's irritated by the delay.'

One of the men grabbed Dom's arm and pulled him from the room.

Dom resisted but the man was too strong. 'Where are you taking me? What's the harvesting programme?'

The man didn't answer. Squirming only made him pull harder. He bundled Dom into an open-sided car. The brightness of the outside hurt his eyes, as if he hadn't seen daylight for some time.

The car took them a few minutes by road to a building on the west side of the city. Dom's eyes watered in the dazzling sunlight. Through the tears, he absorbed as much of Praesidium as he could. He'd never been to the capital city before, but he knew it from the bright, white, sterile look.

The car pulled up outside a building marked "Medical Facility". One of the men got out and dragged him inside. They entered an elevator and rode it down one floor. Dom couldn't tell if they were on the lowest level or if there were more floors. There were no buttons inside the elevator; the man had controlled it by pressing his wrist to a plain panel.

The elevator doors opened and the man pulled Dom along a lengthy corridor with multiple doors on either side. He opened one of the doors to reveal a plain white room. It had a single bed on one side and a chair on the other. The man pushed Dom inside and left.

Dom ran to the door just as it was being locked from the outside.

'Wait! What is this place? Why am I here?'

He banged on the door but the sound of footsteps carried away. He tried the handle next, but it wouldn't budge. He searched the room. No obvious cameras. No windows. No way out except through the one door, which had a small food hatch at the bottom.

A few moments later, the hatch opened and someone slid a food tray across the floor. Dom kicked it away, spilling what looked like a bowl of porridge. He lay down on his stomach and put his face up to the hatch. He slipped his hand through just as it was being closed. A man knelt down and a pair of eyes, cold and lifeless, stared back at him.

'Take your hand out of the hatch space unless you want to lose it.'

'Tell me why I'm here. What is this place?'

The dead expression in the man's eyes didn't change. 'You humans are weak, susceptible to emotions, and the Collective hadn't expected you to survive. Up until now, its focus was on adapting machines to accept human parts. But your acceptance of Praesidium tech has given it another option. You will be its new toy, its new experiment.'

Why did Dom feel like he'd already been that?

'What are you talking about?'

The cold-eyed man continued. 'The Collective has been trapped inside Praesidium for too long. It wishes to live beyond its confines and you're here to help it achieve that goal.'

Dom pulled his hand back and the hatch closed with a snap. He backed up until he hit the wall. Pulling up his top, he examined the ragged scars he had lived with for so long. Thoughts of Carlo infected his mind, and how he'd disappear for a month after each of Dom's operations. Had his father been paid for his permission to use his son as a guinea pig? Déjà vu hit him, like he'd already had that thought.

Dom yelled. 'What is this place?' The sound bounced off the walls.

His memories increased in strength. The name Anya returned to him; she was someone he used to know. He'd seen her in the holding room, but he didn't remember her. And she didn't remember him. But the fog lifted slowly.

More memories returned to him in dribs and drabs. Arcis had been a trap all along. He'd been in there to find out more about why it needed the participants. That information eluded him.

Just five had made it through the final test: the giant machine.

The Collective. He'd heard that name before, just not how or in what context. What did it want with him? Would it ever let him go?

Quintus was another name. A ringleader?

The men in the holding room said his copy didn't take, because of the tech inside him. He pulled up his top and examined the silvery scars. He'd hated them for so long, but they'd ended up saving him from a fate unknown.

Dom frowned at the spilled food on the floor.

Resist.

That's what he'd been taught by Max to do. It's what he would do in this place. Because Dom's anatomy had put a dent in the Collective's plans to copy him. Revealed a weakness in their unbreakable chain of events.

He was valuable to them.

And if Dom sat there long enough, maybe he could work out how to exploit that.

The Rebels

Eliza Green

WARREN HUNT

The Rebels

1

Warren Hunt's parents had taught him only one lesson in his seventeen years: never show weakness. Jean and Philip Hunt had both lived by that rule. One a teacher, the other a farmer. Both highly respected in their fields of expertise. Both admired by the townspeople they lived alongside. But for Warren, he hadn't mastered the skill yet.

So when he'd bumped into Anya in Southwest Essention, he'd suggested an alliance with her. It's what his parents would have done, to strengthen their position in Arcis. The training facility was filled with orphans. Warren wasn't like them. His parents weren't dead. They'd just abandoned him.

Arcis didn't seem to care about that detail.

His whole life, he'd been surrounded by people telling him what to do, how to live. How perfect his parents were and how lucky he'd be if he achieved half of what they had. Jean and Philip had pushed him to become a man, to stand up for what he believed in. They just didn't stick around long enough to see if he'd done it.

Warren didn't feel the same relief as the others after he was brought to Essention and, eventually, Arcis, to mop floors for four creepy wolves. The place had been all anyone could talk about in his town. The urbano and facility, both built by Praesidium, brought renewed hope to the region. It meant the city was interested in the area. That could lead to better farming equipment and bushier crops, some had said.

For Warren, the place was a means to an end. His parents had warned him not to trust the city, and places like Arcis teemed with dangerous secrets. Warren knew his only way to find those secrets would be with an ally.

But Anya's resistance to his idea of teaming up only made him angry. He clenched his fists and controlled his breathing.

'Um, Tahlia told me your parents joined the rebellion,' said Anya.

Warren kicked a stone ahead of him, to keep from yelling.

'I didn't know Tahlia was so interested in my life. What else did she say?' Anya didn't respond. 'That's what I thought. Some bullshit about me in school, no doubt.'

'Um, Jerome and Frank are nice.'

She tried to change the subject. He didn't need her pity.

Warren shrugged. 'I think sometimes they'd rather I wasn't around.'

'Why?'

Was she blind? 'It's a guy thing. I'm not into fighting as much as they are, despite what people say.'

'Well, that shouldn't matter. You're part of the group. Tahlia and June like you.'

'June, maybe. Tahlia's never been my number one

fan.'

'Why?'

'She seems to think of me as this dick who goes around beating people up.'

'Because of the girl and the race?'

Warren's blood boiled. 'She told you about that? It was one time. *God*, she doesn't forget anything. She's labelled me this over-competitive freak who will do anything to get ahead.' He stopped walking. 'I'm just trying to survive, like everyone else.'

Why couldn't she see that? His parents had abandoned him for some stupid rebel cause he knew nothing about.

Ω

During his shift the next day, Warren pretended to be interested in what Jerome and Frank had to say. But mostly, he replayed his and Anya's conversation in his head.

At the end of his shift, he waited for Tahlia outside the changing room. She gave him a strange look when she came out.

'What do you want, Warren? You know it's creepy to hang around the female changing room.'

She logged off at the console in the lobby and exited Arcis. He stuck with her.

'Stop following me.'

'I need to talk to you.'

She passed through the force field surrounding Arcis, then stopped and turned. 'What about?'

'About what you're saying to people about me. You need to stop it.'

Tahlia folded her arms. 'Or what? You gonna tell on

me? You gonna beat me up? I may be short, but I'm strong and not afraid of you.'

Warren stepped closer. He towered over her by at least six inches. Tahlia flinched, but held her nerve.

He pulled her off the street and under the stilts of the Monorail. 'I want to talk to you. I want to know what your problem is with me.'

Tahlia laughed. 'What's *my* problem? You were a shit to me in school. Or don't you remember?'

He frowned. 'When?'

'When I was trying to impress Billy Swanson and you told him the reason I was so small was because I was deformed. Or when I tried to get in with a bunch of girls who were more popular than me, and you told them I had a rare disease that was transmitted through touch. They called me "Scabby Skin" for the rest of the year.'

Warren smiled. 'Oh yeah, I remember now. The looks on their faces when you touched Francesca's arm! She scrubbed her skin raw until it bled.'

Tahlia folded her arms. 'I didn't think it was funny.'

His smile dropped away. 'Well, maybe you don't remember why I started all those rumours.'

'No, because I didn't do anything to you.'

It was Warren's turn to laugh. 'So it wasn't you who told Coach Dewson about my bed-wetting? He said I couldn't run track because he was afraid I'd piss myself.'

Her eyes widened. 'I didn't know you had trouble with bed-wetting.'

'I didn't!'

'So what's the problem?'

Warren grabbed clumps of his hair. 'Are you seriously going to play dumb? You told lies about me.'

'So did you!'

'And now you're telling Anya about me tripping up

that girl in school? She thinks I'm a dick.'

Tahlia uncrossed her arms and slowly nodded. 'Ah, that's what this is about. You like Anya.'

Not in the way Tahlia suggested, but if he mentioned his proposition of an alliance with her, he was certain she'd attempt to undo all his good work.

'No, I just don't appreciate you telling strangers things about me that aren't true.'

Tahlia lifted a brow. 'So you didn't trip up that girl then?'

Warren paused. 'Well, yeah I did, but I didn't mean it.'

Tahlia sighed. 'I still don't know why you needed to talk to me about this. Why do you care what people think of you in Arcis? You don't mix with anyone. You're a loner.'

'I don't mix because I've got better things to do than listen to you and June waffle on about your stupid town lives.'

'And what's so stupid about them? You're from the same town as me. Oakenfield has been good to us.'

'Like Praesidium has been good to you and your family?'

Tahlia stared at him. He'd hit a nerve.

She stormed out from under the stilts and headed down a road leading away from the Monorail station. Warren followed. 'What, you didn't think I knew you were there? Half the town knew. You know what the townspeople said? That your parents were kicked out of Praesidium because you couldn't cut it as an artist. That was the only reason they took you there. Praesidium wanted to study you, study your skills. And in exchange, they promised them money. But the money never came, and they had to return to Oakenfield with their tails between their legs.'

Tahlia stopped walking and turned round. 'We weren't kicked out. We left of our own free will.'

'My father said nobody ever leaves Praesidium of their own free will. They stay there forever or they get kicked out.'

'If you must know, Dad needed to return to Oakenfield to take care of some business. It was a mutual agreement.'

'What business?'

'I don't know. He didn't say.'

Warren folded his arms, feeling smug.

Tahlia leaned in and lowered her voice. 'I know your parents abandoned you. They joined the rebellion. They left you behind because you were weak. You've always been weak. You bully people to get your own way, but that's not power. That's fear.'

Warren's anger surfaced and his chest heaved. How dare Tahlia say that about him? His parents had taught him how to be strong.

So why did they leave you behind?

'I'm not afraid of you, Warren,' said Tahlia.

Warren stepped into her space once more. 'You should be. I won't let you get away with talking shit about me.'

'But it's okay for you to say hurtful things to me?'

'Yes, if they're true.' He tried to control his fast breaths.

Tahlia looked at Arcis and its dual majestic black towers. 'So what are you gonna do to me in Arcis, Warren? We're surrounded by cameras. There are giant mechanical wolves patrolling the ground floor.'

Warren turned to leave. 'Just wait, Tahlia. It will happen when you least expect it.'

2

It had been two days since Tahlia had received an electric shock that put her in the infirmary. Warren had asked Yasmin if she'd heard anything about her condition, but she hadn't. He'd even asked the first-floor supervisor. The man did little more than shrug.

Warren stared at the file in his hand, the one he'd just scanned at his terminal to beat the clock and to avoid getting a shock of his own. Seeing Tahlia frozen to the spot like that had terrified him. The scanner she'd gripped too tight had acted as the conduit for the electricity.

Why hadn't she dropped it? His thoughts went back to their last conversation and where he'd threatened her. Just to scare her off, not to hurt her. When Yasmin had suggested they target the slowest in the group, he'd jumped on the idea. Warren needed to progress and Tahlia would help him whether she wanted to or not.

Tahlia had to be fine. Why wouldn't she be? So what if the task on the first floor delivered a shock? Nobody got hurt, not really. The shocks rattled your body and shook your mind, but they didn't kill you. He dropped his file into a box at the side of the terminal.

It was three days ago when he'd overheard the male

and female supervisor talking about how Arcis would rotate everyone on the first floor if someone was consistently last. How was it his fault that Tahlia had been the slowest?

Karma. For all the nasty rumours she'd spread about him in Oakenfield and here.

He convinced himself she'd been asking for it.

The bell signalled the end of the working day. Warren headed to the dining hall to get dinner. He and the other first-floor participants had been ordered to live on the premises. Not that it mattered to him. All that waited outside these four walls was a cold and empty living unit.

Inside the hall, spirits flagged, including his own. Anya was biting her thumb at the counter. Yasmin and the others in her group looked contrite, as though they now regretted their actions of targeting Tahlia. Okay, so he'd suggested Tahlia, but they'd come up with the plan.

He knew how these things went, how guilt was passed around. There was no way he'd take the fall for this one.

Warren selected his dinner and sat with Anya, June, Frank and Jerome. The mood at the table, plus his own guilt, gnawed away at him. Anya played with her food. June looked around the room, sharp and focused as usual in her observations. Jerome was his quiet self and Frank, normally so vocal, ate in silence.

Warren hated this. He needed to do something to stop the ache in his stomach.

'What do you think about Praesidium?' he said.

Anya looked up. 'What about it?'

'Do you think the city really has the best tech there, or is that all bull?'

'Who cares about Praesidium right now?' said June. 'Tahlia's in the infirmary and we haven't heard anything about her.'

'Yeah, I know. I'm worried for her, too,' said Warren.

Anya shot him a surprised look.

Warren knew what Anya thought of him and that she blamed him. Yet, she'd made the choice to target Tahlia when Yasmin had told her to.

'What tech do you think the city has?' asked Frank.

Warren shifted round in his chair, grateful for Frank's limitless curiosity.

'I don't know. I hear the medical equipment the city uses is top of the range. Like when you get a cut, it can heal you in an instant.'

Jerome scoffed. 'That doesn't sound useful.'

'Why?' said Frank. 'Just because you've never been sick a day in your life doesn't mean the rest of us couldn't use a helping hand.'

Anya seemed to be only half-listening.

Frank turned to Warren. 'Say you have a car accident and your leg is mangled in the crash. Can the city make it as good as new?'

'I've heard its equipment can completely re-engineer the cells, bone, skin tissue,' said Warren. 'It would be like you'd never been injured.'

'How long does it take to heal?'

'A couple of days for bigger injuries.'

Jerome blew out a breath. 'Sounds like science fiction to me. If the city really has that kind of tech, why haven't we seen it in the towns?'

Warren caught June pretending like she wasn't listening.

'Because the towns only ever get the cast-off tech,' said Frank. 'My uncle said Praesidium is huge. The size of six towns put together. He said the place is one giant computer. Every facet, every component, is wired to each other. He said it has underground lairs where the people in charge conduct experiments on people.'

'Why?' said June joining the conversation.

Frank shrugged. 'To figure out what makes them tick. I don't know.'

June laughed. 'And why would they do that?'

'Yeah, sounds a bit far-fetched if you ask me,' said Jerome.

Warren had heard the same story from his rebel-obsessed parents. He'd dismissed most of their crazy stories as hyperbole. That was until the day they left.

'Tahlia lived in Praesidium for a while,' said Warren.

Everyone at their table stopped eating. Anya looked up.

'What did she say about it?' said Frank.

'Not much. That it was white, bright and clean.'

'So?' said Anya. 'We know that, already. We've all been there on our mandatory school trips to the library.'

'That was different,' said Frank. 'The officials brought us straight to the library, then home. We never saw the rest of the city.'

'And did she see any of this amazing tech you say the city's supposed to have?' said June.

'No. But her parents were kicked out of the city. I don't know what happened.'

'Maybe you should wait until Tahlia is here to speak for herself, Warren,' said Anya.

'I wasn't being mean, Anya. I was just saying.'

'Yeah, well, I think your timing sucks.' She stared at her food, her mouth a thin line.

Frank elbowed Warren. 'Don't mind her. I want to hear more about what Tahlia saw and didn't see.'

The ache in Warren's belly grew. Anya was right about the timing.

'She didn't say anything else. Sorry.'

Frank groaned and sat back in his chair. The silence at the table resumed.

After a short while, Warren spoke again. 'I only mentioned Praesidium because it built Essention and runs Arcis. If the city has the tech to heal injuries so fast, then Tahlia will be okay.'

'There's no reason why she shouldn't,' said Jerome. 'I mean, we've all received shocks before and we're all fine.'

'Plus there's the injection they give you to counter the effects of the electric shock,' said Frank. 'The first aiders gave it to Tahlia. I saw them. She was awake when they took her out of the room.'

Yasmin and the others had turned to the conversation.

'Has anyone tried to see her?' said Yasmin.

'I have,' said June. 'I asked the supervisor if I could visit her. He said he'd see what he could do, but he never came back to me after that. If she's still up there tomorrow, I'm going to ask again.' Their access cards no longer worked to activate the elevator. Without a pass, they couldn't leave the first floor.

'Well, maybe I'll come with you. See how she's doing,' said Yasmin.

Anya glared at Yasmin, then down at her plate.

Warren had overheard the supervisors talk about rotation and a last-place participant. It was Yasmin who'd told Anya to mess up Tahlia's chances to succeed, but not before Warren had put the idea in her head. Up until now, Anya had been helping Tahlia to avoid the shocks. Then, after one word from Yasmin, Anya changed her tactics and slowed Tahlia down. They'd all played their part.

Compliance: The wonder drug that messed with peoples' minds and made them controllable. But what the drug didn't do was repress feelings of guilt. It only pushed it further into the background. But it was still there.

'What if she doesn't make it?' said Anya.

'She will,' said Jerome. 'I have a good feeling about it.'

3

Tahlia was dead; the supervisor had announced it just before rotation. The news had hit him like a slow moving train.

But maybe it hadn't been for nothing. He got a rotation out of it.

Cheap shot, Warren. Real cheap.

But this rotation brought with it new rules. He, Yasmin, June, Jerome and Frank had been sent to the second, but Anya had been rotated to the third. Then the supervisor returned, decided he'd made a mistake with Frank, and bumped him up to the third. He hadn't known where Anya had gone until he'd seen her follow the first-floor supervisor across the third floor walkway.

His separation from his only ally in Arcis unnerved Warren. And it bothered him that others were getting bumped up the floors. How could he get in on that? The participants were supposed to experience each of the floors. If he'd known it was possible to skip floors, he'd have asked about it at the last rotation.

With Anya gone, Warren felt his mind slipping to that place where he never felt good enough. But people were pairing off and if he was to fast track his journey to the ninth floor, where his parents said all the secrets were held, Warren needed to regroup and find another ally.

He stood in the second-floor changing room surrounded by hooks on the wall that held white overalls. The female supervisor had instructed them to change. He pulled on a boiler suit that smelled like stale sweat. Dressed, he entered the next room with a stack of green boxes with white crosses on it against one wall. The supervisor stood by an old TV. He picked one up and walked over to where she waited.

'Familiarise yourself with the contents,' she said and hit play. An instructional video on how to administer first aid started.

The five-minute video ended and the supervisor pointed to a set of bulky white manuals.

'Take one on your way out.'

Armed with the thick binder under one arm and his green box in one hand, Warren crossed the walkway and entered a new dorm with overhead lights that pinched at his eyes. He tossed everything on one of the beds and sat down. Others did the same.

The mood in the room had an odd vibe to it: tension, relief—expectation? Nobody had expected Tahlia to die, least of all Warren. They'd only discussed the advanced medical tech belonging to Praesidium the day before—tech that could heal any injury fast. So why couldn't Arcis save Tahlia?

Yasmin studied her manual, wiping away an errant tear. He didn't know if she was sad for Tahlia or for being stuck inside Arcis. She didn't know Tahlia, not like he did.

June was checking out her surroundings, while Jerome was off in his own little world. He did that often, slip into a trance of sorts, except when Frank was around; then he was like a whole new person. Warren sized up

Yasmin, June and Jerome, wondering who out of the three would help him achieve his goals.

The supervisor had told them to wait for the first call. An hour later, there was still nothing.

'I'm hungry,' said June, standing up. 'If anyone's looking for me, I'll be in the dining hall.'

She walked out. Warren watched her go.

'Me, too,' said Jerome, and followed her. Warren shrugged and swapped his boring manual and the dorm for social conversation and food. The others followed soon after.

Yasmin's entire group, six people who'd been through the first floor once and passed over for rotation, had made it to the second floor. Those left behind on the first floor were participants who had rotated from the ground floor at the same time as Warren, Jerome, June, Tahlia, Frank and Anya.

The group hierarchy that had existed on the floor below dissolved on this one. Everyone sat at the same table. With the competitive element removed, there appeared to be no need for the separation. Warren conceded to the reality that they were now on equal terms.

'I can't believe she's dead,' said one of the girls from Yasmin's group.

'You didn't even know her,' said Yasmin.

Warren snorted. 'Neither did you.'

'I knew her.'

'Yeah?' said June. 'Well, both of you can just shut up about it. Yasmin, I know your group approached Anya and asked her to slow Tahlia down. And Warren, I know you were there, encouraging her.'

'What the hell do you know about it?' said Yasmin.

June sat up straighter. 'If Tahlia was someone you claimed to know, you wouldn't have put her in that position in the first place. I mean, what were you both thinking, using Anya like that? And using Tahlia to improve your chances of rotating?'

'I didn't think she would die,' said Yasmin. 'I thought it would play out the way it always has. One person takes the hit and the rest of us benefit from the clock time remaining static.'

June's eyes widened. 'So this strategy was about preserving the clock on the terminal?'

'Yeah. Or didn't you notice how the time decreased when we all made it back on time? Arcis was playing with us.'

'So you decided to turn the tables? By cheating?'

Yasmin banged the table with her fist. 'It's not cheating. It's called *strategising*. Tahlia was the weakest. In the last rotation, a girl called Brianna was the weakest. The supervisors mentioned it because they wanted us to use our brains.'

June stiffened. 'Wait. What? This has happened before?'

'Yeah, last rotation,' said Yasmin softer than before. 'Brianna got caught up the same way. Some of us missed rotation because we didn't figure out the game fast enough.'

'And how did you know to "strategise" the last time?' said June, her voice returning to normal volume.

'We overheard the supervisors talking about rotating everyone if someone finished last.'

'So you essentially overheard the same conversation as Warren?'

'Yeah.'

June shook her head. 'And it never occurred to you that they were setting us up? Mentioning the same strategy twice in two separate rotations?'

Warren's fork froze midway to his mouth.

Yasmin leaned forward. 'Look, we never meant for her to die, but our group's plan was always to rotate. We couldn't endure the shocks for another full rotation. You can't understand if you haven't been overlooked for a rotation. We did what we needed to survive.'

June responded with a rude noise, and shoved her food around the plate with her fork. Warren resumed eating and watched the interaction play out. They both made good arguments. But who would be a better ally: sensible June or risk-taking Yasmin?

He supposed he could team up with Jerome. But he came off as the more passive of him and Frank. Any alliance would most likely be temporary as soon as he reunited with Frank. Maybe Warren could form an alliance with both Frank and Jerome. But not yet.

Now he needed someone to strategise with, and the competition between June and Yasmin was hotting up.

Ω

The first call came in an hour later: an emergency involving a knife and a clumsy boy. June and Warren were sent to the fourth floor, to a trio of prefabs located in Tower A.

They found the boy waiting alone inside one of the prefabs, screaming and crying from the pain. Warren rushed through the parts of the manual and video he'd memorised, which wasn't much. Something about applying pressure to the deep cut on the boy's hand? He found gauze in his green box and pressed it to the wound. June stitched the wound together using a needle and surgical thread.

While she worked, Warren looked around for the

fancy equipment that healed wounds fast, finding none. June cleaned the blood off the boy, told him to take care of his hand and sent him back to the sixth floor with a couple of painkillers and a bottle of water.

Warren and June walked back to the elevator. On the way, June kept glancing at him.

'What?' said Warren.

'Why did you tell Yasmin about the supervisors' conversation?' said June.

'I thought it would help.'

'Help who? You?'

Warren stopped walking. 'Yeah, me. Who else?'

'Jesus, Warren. Do you ever think about anyone but yourself?'

He'd been an only child. Growing up, there had been nobody else to think about. He'd listened to his parents. Their leaving and absence turned his heart cold. He didn't know if he'd ever feel anything or trust anyone again.

'This isn't school, June. This is the real world. We're in here because our parents are gone. I'm just trying to survive, like everyone else here.' He glared at her. 'Do you think Yasmin was right to secure rotation that way? No. But she saw no other way out. She and the others were desperate. The fundamentals of what she tried to do hold true.'

June folded her arms. Her green box dangled from one hand. 'Okay, so Yasmin had an excuse. She'd been through one missed rotation and she was desperate. What's your excuse?'

He paused.

'I don't like being played for a fool.'

June smirked. 'Was that how Tahlia made you feel? She talked about you, you know. What life was like for her in Oakenfield. You weren't the nicest person to her. She said it was like you carried a grudge around all the time and took it out on her.'

'*Jesus!* You're two-faced, you know that?' Warren pinched his arm, to feel something other than anger. 'You got Tahlia's one-sided view and that's all you need to draw your conclusions?'

June dropped her arms to her side. 'Well, what else is there?'

'Nothing I want to tell you.'

'I'm good a reading people. I know enough about you to work out a few assumptions of my own.'

'So that's enough, is it? These assumptions? You don't even want to hear my side of the story?'

'Is there one?' said June.

Warren pinched his arm again. 'Yeah, but I don't want to tell you.'

'Why not?'

'Because I don't like you.'

June laughed a long throaty laugh. In that instant, the quiet, blonde girl vanished. He'd made wrong assumptions about June Shaw. He wouldn't make the same mistake again.

'Well, the feeling's mutual. So why don't we stay clear of each other, okay?'

Warren pressed the button to call the elevator. 'Suits me.'

The doors opened. As Warren climbed on board, he ruled out June as an ally.

Ω

Three hours later, another emergency announcement played over the intercom calling for two people on the

The Rebels

fourth floor. Everyone had taken turns dealing with small incidents there, but calls from the first floor about electric shocks were streaming in—one every twenty minutes—over the last two hours. With everyone out, that left only Warren and Yasmin.

Warren shrugged at Yasmin. 'I guess that means us.'

They walked to the elevator in silence. Warren prepared for a routine cut, sew and bandage case. Yasmin called the elevator. They climbed in and as soon as the elevator moved, Warren turned to her.

'Do you regret what we did to Tahlia?'

Yasmin looked at him. 'No. Do you?'

'No, but I didn't want her to die.'

'Neither did I, but we had no control over what happened at that terminal. Was it our fault that Tahlia couldn't keep up with everyone else? No.' They stepped out of the elevator and crossed the fourth-floor changing room.

Yasmin continued. 'Was it our fault Arcis ran the power for longer than usual? No.'

'So, you think it would have played out the same way, even if Anya hadn't delayed Tahlia?'

'Don't you?'

They entered the room with the prefabs.

'I don't know. What happened with the other girl, Brianna?'

'She was weak, Warren. She wouldn't have survived this place. What happened, happened.'

'And you don't regret anything, or feel remorse?' Warren wanted to know if he was talking to the real Yasmin, not the one on Compliance.

'Of course I feel remorse. But regret? No. Would I do the same thing again? Yeah. You know why?' Warren shook his head. 'Because it's what I needed at the time. And I can't regret something I needed. How it played out was beyond our control.'

She paused outside one of the prefabs, her hand on the doorknob. A girl's muffled cries filtered through the thick walls.

'We all make choices in life, Warren. Some are good. Some are bad. We didn't kill her. Arcis electrocuted her. Not me. Not you.'

'But we set her up to be electrocuted.'

Yasmin sighed. 'If June's right and the supervisors set us up, it would have happened with or without us.'

She jerked the door open and entered the prefab.

Warren watched the hot-headed girl with no fear of consequences. She was cold, hard—the way he felt at times. But he needed a better ally, someone with more empathy than him; someone who wouldn't abandon him to further her own cause; someone to help him succeed in Arcis, no matter what. While Warren didn't trust Yasmin, she was a more appealing choice than June. But neither of them was the right fit for him.

Only one person could help him. And she was on the third floor with Frank.

4

Warren's stint as a first-aid medic on the second floor lasted just twenty-four hours. He was okay with that. He wasn't cut out for medical emergencies anyway. He, June, Jerome, Yasmin and a few others made it to the fourth, where they swapped their boiler suits for casual clothes that smelled clean.

Maybe this floor would be less physical than the second.

Whatever. All that mattered was he'd skipped the third floor. And that meant one step closer to the ninth and finding the truth about where his parents had gone.

They crossed the walkway to Tower B and entered a space with two cordoned off areas. On the left was the girls' dorm, a corridor-style room behind a glass window front. Beds pointed outwards from the wall to the window. A couple of girls sat on their beds, watching their arrival. The supervisor pointed for the girls to go one way and the boys the other.

Warren and Jerome entered the frosted-glass partitioned space opposite to the girls' dorm. Music and laughing assaulted him the second he opened the door. He looked around to see a small party in full swing; there was a bar with alcohol in one corner of the dorm. Boys swigged beers and downed shots of liquor. A glassy-eyed boy handed Warren and Jerome a beer each. Maybe this floor wouldn't be so bad.

But among the happy drunks were others who appeared to be drowning their sorrows.

He shrugged. Nothing to do with him.

Warren took a long drink. The alcohol softened the edges of his exhaustion. He recognised one face: Ash, a boy he'd befriended on the ground floor. If he could call it that. Ash hadn't even been on the same floor as him, but he'd offered Warren advice all the same. Talked about how people were a means to an end in this place. It was their conversation that had convinced Warren to suggest an alliance with Anya. He hoped she'd made it to this floor.

Warren nodded at Ash, sitting on a sofa near the door. Six empty bottles of beer surrounded him. He had one in his hand, which he raised to Warren without a smile.

Jerome walked the room to look for Frank. His buddy was all he could talk about since rotation was announced. After a few laps of the moderate-sized space, he returned to Warren's side and shrugged. Jerome's mood soured and he downed half his beer in one go.

While the beer tasted good, two hours later the exhaustion hit. Warren checked inside each bedroom area, separated by privacy screens, and slumped onto the first free bed he could find. He was about to turn in for the night when he heard someone new come in.

Warren peered round his privacy screen to see Dom Pavesi enter the dorm. He spoke to no one and crashed on a spare bed. He hadn't spoken to Dom, but he knew his type: arrogant and secretive. A lot like June in many ways.

Warren nestled under the covers as the lights went out.

Ω

The next morning, Warren woke to the sound of Dom and Ash arguing. Both alpha males were clashing over the rules in this place. Ash put Dom in his place fast; Warren had a newfound respect for him. Could Ash be a new potential alliance? Maybe, but something was off about him and he couldn't be sure he wouldn't sacrifice Warren to save his own skin.

No, an ally needed to be someone sympathetic who would save him, even if he messed up.

His hands clenched as he thought of his parents.

Ash called for everyone to get dressed.

'Food in ten, people.' With a second alpha in the room, Ash asserted his dominance fast.

They filed out of the dorm and followed the smell of bacon, sweet pancakes and savoury eggs. Warren's mouth salivated.

On the way there, Dom caught up to Jerome and whispered something in his ear. It must have been big because Jerome backed up from Dom with a 'No!'

'I'm sorry, Jerome. We did everything we could.'

Jerome walked over to the frosted-glass wall of the boys' dorm and punched one of the panels. It rocked but stayed put.

Dom led him back into line. He whispered something else to him that Warren couldn't hear. Jerome looked like he couldn't catch his breath.

Warren slipped back from the pair to stand next to Ash. 'What's going on?' he said.

'Some kid called Frank was killed. It's where Dom

was last night. That's why he was late in.'

The news hit Warren like a punch to the gut. It couldn't be true, not so soon after Tahlia.

No wonder Jerome was upset. Should he go to him? He didn't know Frank all that well. And Jerome was a stranger to him.

Ahead, Jerome crashed through the doors of the dining hall.

Warren slowed his walk. He'd never had anyone close to him die before. Apart from Tahlia. But he could barely stand her. He had liked Frank though.

The scene attracted curious gazes from the others, but mostly the mood was light. Despite the heavy drinking session last night, everyone was alert. Compliance dulled the effects of alcohol. It was the perfect hangover remedy.

Warren entered the dining hall and his stomach rumbled instantly. The food was divided into portions kept behind locked glass covers. Warren saw some of the boys were using the chips in their wrists to open the food coverings.

The girls entered and Warren breathed a sigh of relief when he saw Anya had made it to the floor.

He walked over to her and she gave him a brief hug. A bandage on her lower arm caught his eye and he frowned.

'What happened?'

'An accident. I cut myself.'

The line moved forward.

'Well, you seem to be flying through the floors,' said Warren, smiling. 'Maybe I'll stick with you.'

Anya avoided his gaze, glanced at Dom.

What the hell was that look about?

'Maybe. How was the second floor?'

'Brief. Didn't get to do much. What was on the third

floor?' He didn't know if he should ask about Frank, or about how she really got the cut. Tragedy made him uncomfortable. It was why he joked around.

To his relief, Anya didn't explain much.

'Nothing. It was some sort of maze.'

'A maze?'

'It was less interesting than it sounds, believe me.' Her eyes flickered to Jerome.

The line move forward. He thumbed at it.

'I'd better go before I lose my place.'

'Okay. See you.'

Warren walked away with a sick feeling in his stomach. He could see Anya was upset by Frank's death. But it was more than that. She was being weird around him. And any weirdness threatened his chance at an alliance.

He eyed Dom as he slipped back into line. If he'd said something to her...

The first box presented itself. Warren used his chip to unlock a portion of scrambled eggs, bacon and a slice of buttered toast. He selected a coffee from the machine at the end.

But despite his hunger, the feeling of betrayal wouldn't leave him.

Had Anya found a new partner in Dom—was that it? Without an ally, would the controllers of Arcis single him out like they had done with Tahlia, and possibly Frank? Had Frank's death been an accident?

Had his inability to connect with people made him the weakest link?

No, Dom was a dick to most people, and June could be harsh with her words. Maybe Warren should watch what they did, how they acted.

He sat down at a table with the other boys and

scooped some egg into his mouth. A tall, tanned girl—he'd heard Dom call her Sheila—was having trouble with the food boxes. Warren's food suddenly tasted so much better because of it.

'Why aren't the boxes opening for us?' a thin blonde girl said.

Dom jumped up and walked over to them. 'Probably just a mistake. Let me use my chip to open them.'

Do-gooder. Warren wanted to get up and punch Dom in the kidneys. He'd never hated someone so much in all his life. Not even Tahlia and her big mouth. His first impression of him was on the ground floor. Dom had been waiting in the lobby with the tall girl. The girls all lowered their eyes in his presence. But Dom pretended like he didn't notice.

Bull. Warren knew his type. Guys like him got everything handed to him in life. He pretended to be a cool guy, but truth was Warren had never seen Dom help anyone except himself. Yeah, the dude was a selective dick.

'You're not supposed to help them,' said Ash, standing up.

'They need to eat,' said Dom.

Warren smirked. Yeah, Ash could be a good person to ally with.

Dom ignored him and used his chip to open several boxes. After a few attempts, it stopped working. He stared at Ash. 'Why can't I open more?'

Ash sat back down. 'Because you've used up your rations for the day. It won't work again until tomorrow morning.'

'So what are *their* rations? Surely everybody can spare a box?'

Warren stayed where he was, fork in hand. Jerome

squirmed in his seat, looking ready to do Dom's bidding.

'The more you help them outside of the game,' said Ash, 'the worse you score. Trust me. I've been here one rotation too long.'

'I'm not letting them starve,' said Dom.

Ash laughed bitterly. 'You'll change your mind, trust me. Besides, there are more "official" ways they can earn food.'

'I'm sorry I couldn't do more,' said Dom to the girls. He rejoined his table. The other boys shared their food with him, much to Warren's irritation.

After breakfast, they gathered in the open space between the two dorms. A large screen dominated one wall between the dorms. Warren stood with the boys on one side, the girls on the other, and watched the screen. The female supervisor from the second floor appeared on-screen and explained how the fourth floor worked. Ash was right about it being a game: according to her, they had to earn points to rotate. Warren tuned out from most of the instructions, instead plotting ways to win Anya back. Dom would probably try to get in his way.

Warren and the boys retired to their dorm to play VR games, while Jerome hid away in his bedroom. Game playing was one of the point-scoring activities listed on the notice board in their dorm.

But once again, Warren found himself alone watching while two boys he didn't know stuck VR headsets on. He wandered over to the entrance to Jerome's bedroom and stuck his head in. Jerome was lying on his bed, his arm draped over his eyes.

'Hey, man,' he said. Jerome didn't look up. 'You doing okay?'

Jerome glared at him.

'What do you want, Warren?'

Warren bristled from his sharp tone. Screw him.

'I wanted to say sorry about Frank. I just heard.'

Jerome stood up and pushed past him. 'It doesn't matter.'

Warren grabbed him by the arm as he passed, causing Jerome to turn and glare at him.

He let go. 'Look, if you ever need to talk, I'm here. I knew Frank too. He was my friend.'

'Like Tahlia was your friend?'

'What's that supposed to mean?'

'You pick and choose when you want to be friends and when you don't. Take the dining hall in there. You didn't even get up and help the girls.'

Warren saw red. 'Neither did you.'

'Well, I was going to but—'

'But what? You changed your mind because you would have lost rations?'

Jerome pressed his lips together.

'So why are you picking on me?'

'Because you don't seem to care about anyone except yourself. This place is just a game to you. We're all just a game.' Jerome folded his arms. 'Tell me, when was Frank's birthday? You claim to know him so well, so that shouldn't be a problem for you.'

Warren had no idea. 'I don't know anyone's birthday in here. Does that make me a bad person?'

Jerome sighed and some of the anger visibly drained away. 'No, it doesn't. But you have no idea what I'm going through. Frank was like a brother to me and it feels like you're cashing in on that somehow.'

'I'm not.' Warren stepped forward, lowered his voice. 'What happened to him?'

'An accident with a rotating blade, Dom said.'

'Is he dead?'

Jerome's eyes popped. 'Yes, he's dead! Why would you ask such a thing?'

'It's just that Frank used to talk about Arcis having medical tech. We never got to use any of it while we were first aiders. I thought maybe Arcis had found a way to save him.' Jerome huffed and turned to go. 'I'm sorry. I didn't mean to be—'

Jerome looked back at him. 'Insensitive? Well you are.'

Warren ran his fingers through his strawberry-blond hair. 'I never lost someone like that. I'm new to this. I'm sorry.'

Jerome huffed. 'Look, I know you're trying and I'm sorry for what I said. I just miss Frank, okay?'

'Yeah.' *Whatever.* 'I'll leave you to it.'

Jerome headed for the exit and left, leaving Warren to process his feelings of guilt. Jerome hadn't been wrong with the things he'd said, but it wasn't Warren's fault. Compliance made him act like this. His parents had left him to fend for himself. He was just doing what he could to survive. What was wrong with that?

He looked up to see Ash and Dom in separate sections of the dorm. Both of them were watching him.

5

Oh God, he hadn't meant to take it that far. It was the damn Compliance.

But he couldn't see another way to rotate.

His jaw ached where Anya had just punched him. Shaking with anger, he left her alone in the bathroom and strode back to the male dormitory. Why couldn't she see what he needed? The game required them to get physical. It said so on the notice board. She knew how things worked here. Ash had explained it to her.

He yanked open the door to the dorm, but slowed his walk when he neared Dom's cubicle. Dom was sitting on the edge of his bed, his head bowed and his clasped hands resting the tops of his legs. He looked up, as though he sensed him there. A look of disappointment flashed in his eyes. Warren felt the look all the way down to his non-slip shoes.

He flashed him a weak smile and walked on. Only when he reached his bed and flopped down onto it did he release the tense breath he'd been holding. The lights were still on in the dorm—a couple of the boys continued to play VR by the booze station. Warren got up, grabbed a bottle of scotch from the bar and carried it back to bed.

The Rebels

The alcohol burned his throat and cleared his foggy mind—the opposite of what he wanted. He'd known all about the substance the rebels called Compliance before he'd arrived at Arcis or Essention. His parents had talked about nothing else for months; how it affected the body and mind, and turned people into mindless robots. The alcohol seemed to sharpen his focus, counteract the effects.

He took another long pull from the bottle. His controlled anger subsided, but his shame filled the void. What was he thinking, forcing himself on Anya like that? If Dom ever found out...

The cubicle wall surrounding his bed closed in on him. Something about Dom and Sheila was off. He'd seen them whispering to each other. Did Anya know they'd been together earlier this evening, disappeared to one of the spare rooms at the back of the dorm, stayed in there for fifteen whole minutes? When they had emerged, Sheila had smiled at Dom and given him a peck on the cheek. Warren had wanted to smash his smug face in.

Dom got everything he wanted in life.

Except for Anya.

She had been paired with Jerome, a partnership Warren knew Dom had orchestrated to keep him away. Jerome had stuck to the easier tasks on the list, like slave for the day.

Warren had picked June—she was familiar and less hostile than Sheila. But June had been difficult all day, taking too long to do tasks.

He hadn't planned on hurting Anya. But with June scuppering his chances to rotate, he needed Anya's help more than ever. That day in Southwest when he'd followed her, he had promised her they'd get out of Arcis together. At the time he had meant it.

But now? She was cold and indifferent towards him. She'd been gung ho for the alliance until someone better had come along. Now she and Dom were tight.

She could die in Arcis for all he cared.

He imagined his parents shaking their heads at him. Disappointment.

He blocked out their faces most days, but at night he'd dream about them.

His mother and father's inability to make up their mind had turned Warren's life into an either/or scenario. Choose archery over mathematics. Choose martial arts over art. Stay in Oakenfield or leave for a life on the outside. But before he could give them an answer, they'd abandoned him. The note they'd left was now a pile of ash, but every word would be forever burned into his memory.

Warren swigged more alcohol. He was used to being alone. He didn't play games well, but Arcis had taught him how to fake it. His goal to reach the ninth floor remained his top priority. It was where he believed the coordinates for the Beyond were. His parents had whispered about a place that existed beyond the towns, and that Praesidium knew where it was.

The alcohol soothed his anger and relaxed his tense shoulders. But his shame continued to rage inside him. He dragged a hand down his face. He'd had no right to ask Anya to do that. But June had limited his options.

Warren drank from the bottle that was a quarter empty now. The Compliance in his system reduced the effects of the alcohol too much. He wanted to forget.

Ash appeared at the open entrance to his sectioned-off bedroom.

He leaned against the edge of the cubicle wall. 'Rough day?'

Warren still didn't know what to make of Ash. Most

times he seemed normal, although his act for the girls was too forced for Warren's taste. But he noticed something new, a heavy look to his eyes that hadn't been there before. Ash had picked Lilly. Maybe she'd been as helpful to him as June had been to Warren. He didn't care. The man before him was the perfect person to get drunk with right now.

'It's getting better.' Warren shook the bottle at him. 'You want some?'

Ash walked forward and sat on the edge of Warren's bed. He took the bottle and drank a quarter in one go. He coughed and wiped his mouth with his hand.

Dom looked in as he passed by the partition.

Warren whispered to Ash. 'Come on, there are too many ears here. I want to drink in peace.'

Ash collected another bottle from the bar and carried it to the male bathroom.

He pointed at Warren's jaw. 'Who gave you that?'

'Nobody.' Warren sat on the counter and leaned against the mirror. 'So, what's your excuse for looking like crap?'

Ash was slouched against the wall, full bottle in hand. 'Nothing. I just... I can't be here any more.' He dropped his gaze to the tiled floor. His lips rounded over the top of the bottle and he tipped it back. 'I hate it.'

'Yeah, I hate Arcis, too.'

Ash shook his head as he swallowed. 'Nah, I mean I hate the fourth floor. I need to get off it. I won't go through another rotation. I can't.'

'Yeah, I know what you mean.'

'No, you don't. This place, it turns you into someone else. It gets under your skin, makes you think it's okay to ask for things.' Ash looked away. 'Not ask... More like take things that don't belong to you.' He sucked on the bottle. 'I hate it.'

Warren's mind flashed back to the incident between him and Anya. 'But what if you need those things to, you know, progress?'

Ash laughed bitterly. 'Well, then I guess it's okay.'

'How long have you been in here?'

'Who the hell knows? Two months? Three? I've lost track of time.'

'Where did you come from before Essention?'

Ash smirked at him. 'You want to hear my life story?'

Warren could do with a distraction from this place. 'Sure.'

'There's not much to tell, really. I was like any other kid in a neighbourhood. Then my parents were murdered by rebels. I got sick and I was brought here. Sound familiar?' Warren nodded. 'That stupid rebellion has a lot to answer for.'

Warren agreed. He hated the rebels for stealing his parents away, and for making his parents think he couldn't handle their secret.

Ash looked at him, his gaze sharp. 'What's your story?'

'Nothing much. Same as you.'

'Hey, I heard about what happened with that girl on the first floor. Tahlia something? Did you know her?'

'Yeah, she came from the same town as me.'

Ash sighed. 'Bummer. I heard the electricity did a real number on her.'

'How did you hear?'

'Jerome told me.'

'Yeah, well, she wasn't fast enough to finish.' Warren took a drink.

Ash laughed and sucked on the neck of his bottle

and swallowed. 'That's a little cruel, don't you think?'

'No, I don't.'

'So, people should die because they're slower than someone else? What about their other skills?'

'What are you talking about?'

'What if someone isn't good at running but they're great at strategising? What makes them less than the person built for speed?'

'My parents told me there was only one lesson in life: to be tough.' Warren tipped the bottle back again.

'Really? So what does being "tough" mean?'

Warren gave him a look.

'I'm serious. Is being tough what we see on the outside or the inside? Is it physical or mental strength that matters?'

Warren didn't know any more. 'I used to think it was both.'

'Sometimes it's about knowing when to consider someone else's feelings. Don't get me wrong. Consideration can also get you nowhere and sometimes you have to think about number one. But do you think Tahlia's death helped anyone in here?'

Warren wanted to say it had helped him to rotate, but he'd only wanted to scare Tahlia.

Ash held the bottle out, stared at it. 'I'm not getting any buzz off this. I thought there was supposed to be alcohol in it... At my drinking rate, I should be on the floor, passed out by now.'

Warren didn't mention Compliance. He didn't want it getting back to the controllers. 'Tastes fine to me. I can feel a little buzz.'

'It's not enough. I need to forget.' Ash stared at Warren. 'How are you getting on with June? She making your life easy or hard?'

'Hard.' Warren sighed. 'I don't know if I'll make it to next rotation.'

'Bummer. You'll be okay. You seem strong. You can probably handle another rotation.'

'And you will too, if Lilly's help doesn't get you there.'

A dark look crossed Ash's eyes. 'That's not gonna happen, man. I can't bear to be here another second longer. I hate what this place is doing to me. How it's turning me into an asshole. Can't you feel it, how this place messes with our minds? We're all making choices we shouldn't be making. We're barely adults, what the hell do we know?' He clunked the bottle down on the counter. 'This place is too grown-up for my ass.'

Truth was Warren hadn't felt like a kid for some time. His parents had made sure of that. They didn't want to raise a weak little boy. Strong boys didn't need presents on their birthdays, or ice cream when they were good. Strong boys didn't get praise when they did well on a spelling test. Their tough love was preparation, they had said, for life in the Beyond.

'Oakenfield is just a temporary home,' his father had said. 'Don't get used to it. We might not be here that long.'

'If this isn't home, where is?' said Warren.

'The real world. There, everything is dark and dirty and people say what's on their mind.'

Warren tipped the remaining alcohol into his mouth. He shook the empty bottle at Ash. 'I'm done and off to bed.'

'Yeah, I'm gonna hang here a while longer.'

His walk back to the dorm unsettled him. He imagined Anya sitting on her bed glaring at him. He quickened his step and slipped inside the dorm.

It had been the right thing to do. His efforts would show on the scoreboard tomorrow. When they'd rotated to the first floor, he'd asked Anya, 'Are you sure you don't want a buddy in here?'

She'd replied, 'Your offer's starting to look more tempting by the day.'

He'd taken her reply as sign she'd wanted an alliance. He was only taking what she'd promised him.

So why did he feel so shitty about it?

6

New music thumped and drowned out Warren's thoughts. It couldn't have come at a better time.

He had an Electro Gun and the maze before him contained a bunch of floating discs. What he needed right now was to shoot things.

Seeing Ash fall over the side of the walkway had shocked him. While Ash might not have been a friend, he didn't deserve that. Warren had only been chatting to him hours before. Then Lilly went over the edge. The others had watched it happen. What angered him most was not one of them had tried to pull Ash to safety. But Compliance mellowed out his feelings too soon after.

The clock ticked back from twenty minutes. This place sure did know how to change things up. Fifteen minutes ago, the scoreboard on the fourth floor had shown he'd lost points, not gained them. But that didn't matter, because the supervisor had rotated most of them anyway. Anyone on negative scores hadn't made it.

Warren held his Electro Gun close to his chest as he navigated the fifth-floor maze. He checked the long blue vein on the side of his gun that indicated a full charge.

His game plan was to run a lap of the entire space

within the time allocated. He should be able to find all the black discs that way. The others were on similar solo runs. Several shots rang out close by, their crackle muted by the heavy base of the music.

The timing of rotation had also become less predictable. He'd spent no more than a few days on both the second and fourth floor—a change from thirty days on the ground floor and a similar count on the first. For all he knew, they could call rotation in twenty minutes. Every effort had to count if he was to reach the ninth floor.

The look in Ash's eye haunted him. The dark conversation they'd had last night made sense now. Ash had forced himself on Lilly. And judging by his scores, he'd been successful. What the others didn't know was how in pain Ash had been.

Warren ran down a corridor, taking turns when they allowed. Walls shifted; some blocked his route, others opened up a new one. He stopped and touched the wall, feeling a weird shiver there. He poked a finger into the surface and it yielded half an inch before it firmed up. He couldn't see a strategy. The thumping music reminded him that time was not on his side. As he ran, the heavy base drowned out some of his feelings of shame.

It was only when he saw Anya nursing her arm in the changing room that he realised how rough he'd been with her. Sheila and June had surrounded her like a couple of attack dogs. He hadn't meant to reopen her wound, or to make her hate him. But what's done was done.

The droning music had a chaotic quality that fuelled Warren. He pushed on to complete Arcis' latest game. He managed one last shot before the music stopped and the walls retracted into the floor. The music continued to hum in his ears. Dom had won that round.

Smug bastard.

It was still the middle of the night. They settled in their dorm; boys on one side, girls on the other. Warren kept his distance, keen not to draw attention to his behaviour on the fourth floor. As he pulled a pair of pyjamas out of his backpack, Anya glanced over. He tried to catch her eye, to pass on his apology, but she looked away too fast. Sheila and Yasmin stared at him until he dropped his gaze and focused on his backpack once more.

He'd noticed the little cliques that were forming. It had started on the ground floor: June with Tahlia, Frank with Jerome. It was supposed to be him and Anya. The people may be different but the strategy was the same. And Warren was once again on the outside.

He flung his pyjama bottoms away to the end of his bed and lay down. Closing his eyes, he ran through his plan to reach the ninth floor.

The Compliance in his system made it easy to switch off his emotions. He still felt everything, but in shorter measures. The group made plans without him. It angered him, but with a little concentration he could push it away.

He thought about Ash. He could have been a possible friend.

But this was exactly what his parents had warned him about—not to get attached to places or people. His mother had worked as a teacher in Oakenfield. His green-fingered father had adopted many of Praesidium's ideas and tech in accelerating plant growth. But it had always felt like Jean and Philip Hunt were biding their time, waiting for something better to come along.

Warren had lived his childhood in restless fear. It made growing up difficult, not knowing if he should bother making friends in any one place. Not knowing if his parents would be there when he woke up the next morning.

Then, one day they weren't. The note they'd left explained their decision to leave him behind. One sentence stood out from the rest.

You're not ready to see what we have to show you.

See what, exactly? He'd crumpled the note and set it on fire. Then he'd tried to forget he ever had parents. That day had been coming for a while. He just hadn't prepared for it.

His plan to forget had worked for a month, until he ran out of food and got caught stealing bread. That had been a year ago and he'd been old enough to live by himself.

Warren tuned in to the discussion about tactics. Their exclusion of him tightened his skin. He kept his eyes closed and pretended to sleep.

'So how did you know to shoot the wall?' said Jerome.

'Uh?' said Anya.

'The wall. You said it was organic.'

'I put my hand on it and it didn't feel like a real wall. I was getting turned around so much it felt like the maze was closing me in.'

'And it did, eventually,' said Jerome.

If anyone had bothered to ask Warren, he could have told them he'd already figured that out. Probably before Anya. He opened one eye and saw people rallying around her. Irritation bloomed in his chest. *He'd* been Anya's only friend on the ground floor. Now everyone was shutting him out.

'So, Dom has earned the most points,' said Jerome. 'I guess we keep playing until we have a winner. How many rounds, do you think?'

'Until we pass their test,' said Dom.

Warren looked over at Jerome. With Frank gone, he

was looking like his best bet out of Arcis. He needed someone to have his back, not to stick a knife in it. He shut his eyes again.

'I like Anya's idea of blasting the walls. How many blasts do we get per gun?' said Jerome.

'Fourteen discs, so fourteen shots each,' said Dom.

'Can't we split into teams?' said June. 'We can each take turns to blast the wall, then the disc. The supervisor said we could do it any way we liked.'

'There needs to be a winner.' Even Yasmin—the liar—was part of the gang.

'Why do we need a winner?' Sheila asked. 'Why can't we all finish on the same score and rotate together?'

'Okay, that's possible.' June added her two cents. 'But there are thirteen of us. How do we split the teams?'

'Warren's with Sheila and me,' said Yasmin. His eyes shot open. Yasmin was staring at him.

No. Nope. No way. Yasmin had tried to stick the blame for what happened to Tahlia on him. He would work out his own strategy.

'We need the girls to split up, so it's even,' said Dom. 'The boys are better at navigating the maze.'

The others split the remaining teams without Warren's input.

'Okay, so the strategy is for all of us to finish on the same score,' said June.

That's when Warren tuned out. Compliance made it too easy to push people away. Life in Arcis was no different to his life in Oakenfield. He cared little, expected even less, and trusted nobody.

He didn't bother changing out of his sweaty clothes and climbed under the covers. They could plan and scheme all they wanted, but he would play the game his way.

The Rebels

All that mattered now was locating the Beyond, the place he was sure his parents had gone to; a place they'd said existed beyond Praesidium's control.

And when he got there, he would find his parents and destroy their lives, like they'd destroyed his.

7

Warren's strategy to win on the fifth floor had worked, although he'd paid the price for it with two Electro Gun blasts to the body. Nine of them had rotated after the second run through the maze. They skipped the sixth floor.

Warren hobbled across the seventh-floor walkway. At first he was angry at Anya for shooting him, but it had been worth it to ditch Sheila and Yasmin. Both of them had been slowing him down on purpose, blocking his access to the black discs. But he'd deserved Anya's anger. He just wished he could explain how desperate he'd been, and what was at stake if he couldn't rotate.

Maybe you should have tried talking to her first.

It was all June's fault. She'd acted like a bitch, messing up his chance to earn points. If she'd helped like she was supposed to, he wouldn't have needed Anya.

He entered Tower B and looked around the room that held dozens of, what looked like, dentists' chairs with screens. Twelve participants in total had made it to the seventh floor; nine from the fifth floor and three from the sixth. Warren and Jerome stayed together on one side of the room with two boys from the fifth floor and a boy and girl from the sixth floor. June, Yasmin, Sheila, Dom, Anya and the last boy from the sixth floor were on the other side. The division between the two groups was so wide it might as well have been a chasm.

But his guilt made him desperate to explain his actions to Anya. Maybe if he explained what his parents had done, she wouldn't hate him so much.

He remembered his father telling him about the Beyond. Warren had seen no proof of any place existing beyond the towns or Praesidium, and he'd told him so.

'You're too rigid in your thinking, son. You believe this small-minded town to be your happy ever after. Well, it's not. This world has gone to hell and nobody has a damn clue. Praesidium has made sure of that. Your ignorance will be your undoing, Warren. Your mother and I have tried to explain to you... this world is a fantasy... but you refuse to listen.'

'So tell me what I'm missing. You've been vague about this place,' said Warren. 'Or even better, why not show me?'

His father shook his head. 'Because once I do, there's no coming back to here, to your friends. You understand? It's a one way trip.'

That got Warren's back up. 'Then don't show me. I don't care.' He'd stormed off.

A week later, his parents had left him and he'd found their note.

Warren looked across the divide. Anya was standing off to the side of the chairs, away from the others, but more important, away from Dom. New feelings of remorse hit him. He marched over to her before the tests began, and before Dom noticed.

'Anya. *Please*. I need to talk to you.'

Her eyes widened and she backed away. 'Don't come any closer.'

Dom got between them and stuck his hand on Warren's chest.

'What the hell do you think you're doing?' said Dom.

'Get out of my way, Pavesi. I need to speak—'

'If you take another step towards her, I'll do more than just punch you.'

'Anya, I'm sorry. I just want to explain—'

She looked so frightened. 'No, Warren. Leave me alone.'

Dom pushed him back. 'You heard her.'

Warren let out a frustrated yell and muttered, 'Asshole,' as he walked away.

He stalked back to his chair and sat in it, hard. The female supervisor attached two white circles of fabric to the sides of his head. She explained that when a question popped up on-screen, he should press the blue button on-screen and think his response.

He could give her a response right now.

As the supervisor tended to the others, Warren's anger gave way to strategy. How should he play this game? What questions would Arcis ask? Should he answer truthfully? He had no idea what Arcis even needed from them.

When the questions started out basic enough—what his favourite colour was and what he liked about school—he opted for the truth. A short film played, showing a mother in hospital tending to two sick children. The question was, 'Who would you save?'

Warren answered.

Let the baby and child die. They shouldn't have to live in this crappy world with a selfish mother.

He looked over at Anya who was concentrating on her screen. Dom was glancing at her.

His chest heaved when he looked at Pavesi. The arrogant ass had shouted at him, made a fool of him in front of everyone. Who the hell did he think he was?

People like him needed to pay.

Maybe not now, but soon.

His parents had taught him to act tough even when he didn't feel it, and to gain the upper hand in awkward situations. Ironically, their advice had worked best after they'd left to join the rebellion. That little fact was also in their note.

> *We've gone to offer our help to one of the rebellion factions. We are close to finding the place known only as the Beyond. We would have taken you with us but last night proved you're not ready to see what we have to show you. You're too soft, Warren. You're not strong enough to handle the truth of what lies beyond Praesidium's control. You'll be safer here, in the towns. When we reach the Beyond and figure out how to destroy this place, we'll come back for you. Survive. Be tough. Don't let anyone break you. Burn this note after you've read it.*

After reading it, Warren's first urge had been to show it to all of Oakenfield. But instead, he'd done as they'd asked.

Tough. Unbreakable. That's who Warren had to be to survive in this world. He hated the rebellion—its very existence was why he was alone. If there was a rebel in the room right now, he'd kill him or her.

In a way, Warren was a different kind of rebel.

Anya gasped suddenly and his gaze went to her. She tugged the dots free from her head and bolted from her chair towards the dorm. Dom followed her just as the supervisor came into the room and told everyone to take a break.

Warren peeled the white dots off his head and got out of the chair. In the dining hall, he got food and a bottle of water and looked around at the collection of people—new and old. There was still time to make new alliances. Jerome sat alone while the two boys from Jerome's old team on the fifth floor and the two boys and girl from the sixth floor chatted with each other.

Perfect.

He slid into the seat next to Jerome. 'Hey, how are you doing, you know, after Frank?'

Jerome looked up at him. His eyes were a little brighter than before. 'I haven't had much time to process it. I'm grateful we've been kept busy.'

Warren drank some water. 'So, you ready to get out of this place?'

'Yeah, I can't stand being here any more. It's getting to me.'

'I was hoping you'd say that. I was thinking we could pair up, strategise a little? I know you and Frank were tight on the floors below, but I can be a good replacement for him.' He tried to look contrite. 'Sorry to be so insensitive.'

Jerome smiled. 'Yeah, Warren. It's cool. I don't think you're being insensitive. And I was actually thinking the same thing about pairing up with someone. Hey, what's going on with you and Anya?'

Warren rubbed the back of his neck. 'A misunderstanding. She was supposed to be my buddy in here, but she changed her mind.'

Jerome scooped some egg into his mouth. 'It's none of my business. This place has made everyone crazy. I'm sure you'll sort it out when we finish the programme.'

'Yeah, that's what I was thinking. Everything will be fine once we leave here.'

Jerome poked him in the arm. 'And I saw how Sheila and Yasmin have been with you. I don't like that clique-y crap. Just so you know.'

Warren shrugged. 'That's girls for you, right?' He tipped back his bottle of water.

Jerome laughed a little. 'Yeah. I hated how they went on sometimes at my school.' He leaned closer. 'Hey, what happened to your parents, anyway?'

Warren swallowed too much water and coughed.

'Sorry, I didn't mean to bring it up. It's just that Tahlia said—'

'Tahlia never could mind her own business.'

Jerome held up his hands. 'Sorry, man. None of my business, either.'

Warren considered telling him straight. It might build a little trust between them.

'Nah, it's okay. They left. I woke up one morning and they were gone.'

'What, no note?'

'Nothing.'

'Sorry. That's rough.'

Warren shook off his irritation with a shrug. 'What about you?'

Jerome ruffled his short hair. 'I don't remember my parents. I went to live with Frank's uncle—that part you know. Nothing more to tell, really.'

'No brothers or sisters?'

'Only child. Frank was like a brother to me.'

'Sorry.'

Jerome shrugged. 'No biggie. My story's a little bland in comparison to everyone else's. Sometimes I think I should make up something just to fit in.'

'Nah, bland works just fine.'

The supervisor came to get them and the tests resumed in the next room. Anya returned to her seat looking more composed than before.

The second round of questions started off more specific than the first round. Nothing too personal. Warren answered them honestly.

But the fourth question threw him for a loop.

'If one had to die, whom would you kill?' A photo of his mother and father accompanied the question.

He hit the blue button on-screen and thought of his response. *Both*.

It was how he felt right at that moment.

'Why do you hate your parents?'

Because they abandoned me.

'Where did they go?'

I don't know.

'Did they join the rebels?'

I don't know.

'Is there a rebellion movement nearby?'

I don't know.

'Are they planning an attack on Arcis?'

I don't know.

'Do you think there are rebels in Arcis right now?'

I don't know.

'Why are you avoiding our questions, Warren?'

I can't answer your questions.

'If you don't answer them properly, we will detain you here.'

Okay, fine. I don't think there are rebels in Arcis. I

hate my parents for leaving me behind. They didn't tell me where they were going.

The screen went blank and the supervisor returned to the room. Warren pulled the white circles from his head. 'The first five people on this side of the room have made it to the next level.'

Anya, Dom, Yasmin, June, Sheila.

Sheila released a quick breath. The boy from the sixth floor in Anya and Dom's group had missed out on rotation.

'The rest of you will take the test again.'

Jerome punched his chair. Warren folded his arms. Anya glanced over with a look of pity. She could keep it. Dom, on the other hand, had a stupid grin on his face.

Warren, Jerome and the rest of the retakers were told to wait in the dining hall. Anya and the others followed the supervisor out of the room.

Warren couldn't believe he'd missed out on rotation. What had he done different to Dom?

'What the hell happened? Why are we being kept back?' he said.

'No idea,' said Jerome. 'I answered the questions the way I thought I was supposed to.'

'Are there right or wrong answers?' said one of the boys. 'Is that why we're still here and the others have rotated? Because we answered the wrong way?'

'It's hard to say,' said Jerome. 'Some of the open-ended questions were so vague, it was impossible to know.' He sat back and groaned. 'How the hell does this floor work?'

Warren sat up straight. 'The supervisor said we get to do the test again. So next time we answer them differently. See if that changes the result.'

Jerome nodded. 'Okay. I'm up for trying that.'

8

The supervisor didn't return straight away. Warren, Jerome and the remaining four boys and one girl, whose names he hadn't bothered to ask, entertained themselves in the dining hall. Warren grabbed one of the dinner knives and convinced the others to play his favourite game. All the person had to do was splay their hand out flat on the table while he stabbed between the fingers with a knife. The girl started the timer and the boys played.

'The first person to flinch loses,' said Warren. He'd played this game once before, on the first floor. Jerome had surprised him by holding out the longest.

The first boy flinched almost immediately. He swapped seats with Jerome.

'Careful with that damn knife,' said Jerome as Warren stabbed between his fingers. Despite his protests, Jerome kept his nerve, never flinching once.

Warren had practised the game many times alone, but playing against an opponent made it more interesting. He'd played it in school against kids he suspected to be children of rebels. His theory? If they flinched, they were too weak to be connected to the rebellion. Everyone did in the end, but he got a kick out of scaring them anyway. And sometimes, on purpose, he nicked the fleshy part in between the fingers.

Another of the nameless boys was up next. He splayed his hand out, but as Warren stabbed in between his fingers, the boy's breathing quickened to the point where Warren thought he might pass out.

One centimetre to the left and the sharp knife would puncture the skin. Warren resisted the urge to test this kid's resolve. Weak people were either losers or wound up dead, like Lilly. If Lilly had been a stronger person, she would have seen that Ash had been trying to get them both to the next level. If she hadn't flipped out, Warren could have had a choice of either Ash or Jerome as an ally.

He upped the tempo, increased the speed of the knife. The boy started to sweat.

He wasn't sure what drove him to push this kid. The boy never took his eyes off the knife and neither did Warren, except to check on the kid's status. When the boy looked ready to give in, the door opened and the supervisor appeared. The boy slid back his hand and let out a long sigh.

'Please follow me. The test is about to recommence.' The supervisor left the room.

'That doesn't count as a win,' said Warren to the boy. 'On the next break, we go again.' The blood drained from the boy's face and Warren smirked.

On the way back to his chair, he noticed the supervisor looked more nervous and less confident than before the last round of tests. He eyed the layout of the room and the seven remaining participants. Just them. Nobody new. The lack of new participants was a deviation from every other rotation. What was different this time round?

He sat in the chair and thought about his new

strategy to get off the seventh floor. The supervisor attached the dots to his head and he closed his eyes, breathing in deep. Had his unwillingness to answer questions about his parents' whereabouts held him back? Why did Arcis want to know so bad?

Because it has expressed concern about increased rebel activity in the area and it thinks you're a rebel, too.

It had to be why Arcis had asked if he'd thought rebels were in the building. The controllers wanted him to confess.

Warren settled into the chair. He would pick a different answer if Arcis asked him again. He would tell the controllers what they wanted to hear, that his parents were rebels, and they'd left a note.

With the white circles in place on his head, Warren resumed his test. The first question appeared on the screen.

'What would you be doing right now if your parents were still in Oakenfield?'

Warren pressed the blue button and thought his response.

I would probably be doing chores. They were strict.

'Why were they strict with you?'

Warren shifted in his chair. *I don't know.*

'Unacceptable answer. Were you a bad child?'

No. They were just strict, that's all. Like a lot of parents in Oakenfield.

'Why do you think that is?'

I don't know.

'Unacceptable answer. Where have your parents gone?'

It would be easy to tell Arcis about the Beyond, or the rebel stronghold his parents had mentioned some time ago, located somewhere in the mountains.

I told you, I don't know.

But it was easier to lie.

New text appeared on the screen.

'You must know where they've gone. You are their only child. Have they travelled beyond the safe zone?'

The safe zone? I don't know what that is.

'Did they leave you a note?'

Warren gripped the arms of his chair.

No.

'You're lying. Your adrenaline has just spiked.'

No, I'm not.

'Then why has your heart rate suddenly elevated?'

Warren thought fast and clutched his stomach.

I feel sick. Sometimes the bread makes me queasy. I think I have an intolerance to wheat.

'Did your parents travel beyond the safe zone?'

I don't know anything about a safe zone. Stop asking me.

'Unacceptable answer. Tell us the truth or you will receive a shock.'

I don't know anything about a safe zone. I swear. My parents didn't tell me jack about what they were doing or not doing. You're wasting your time with me.

A snap of electricity, delivered through the circles attached to his head, jerked him sideways.

Stop! I'm telling you the truth.

'What did the note say?'

There was no note.

Another shock hit him. Warren clenched his teeth.

'We can keep this up all day. What did the note say?'

We?

I don't know—

Another shock cut off his thoughts. He growled in pain.

Okay! It said I wasn't ready to see what they wanted to show me.

'And what did they want to show you?'

Hell if I know. They didn't tell me anything.

A pause followed. 'We believe you, Warren. You may think our methods to be cruel, but we are just protecting you from harm. From a serious threat to our survival, and yours.'

What threat? The rebels?

'You must endure the shocks for a little longer. We are not finished with our questions. If you tell us the truth, we will not need to use force—'

A sudden loud rattle shook through the ceiling and then the floor. Warren's screen went blank.

'What the hell was that?' said Jerome looking around. Warren looked up at the ceiling, worried it might collapse in on them.

The supervisor relocated from the corner to the middle of the room. She looked up at the ceiling as well, confused.

'Continue with the tests. I'll check it out.'

She headed for the exit and walkway, and disappeared through the door.

'Screw this,' said Warren, peeling away the circles. He didn't want to wait in a room that could cave in at any moment.

'What happened to you during the test?' said Jerome. 'You looked like you were in some serious pain.'

'The controllers shocked me. Said I wasn't answering their questions to their liking. I'm not staying here to get shocked again.'

Jerome pulled off his own circles. The others did the same. 'Shocked, why? What sort of questions was Arcis asking you?'

The Rebels

He played it down. 'The usual. Nothing important. Hey, how about we find a way off this floor?'

'Yeah, I wanna go home,' said one of the boys. The girl nodded.

'The rest of you can do what you like,' said Warren. 'But I'm heading up. I came here to reach the ninth floor.' He couldn't turn back now, not when he was this close to finding out where his parents had gone.

'Well, if you're going up, then so am I,' said Jerome marching away. 'Come on, let's try the elevator.'

Warren smiled and followed Jerome out of the test room; the supervisor had left the door unlocked. They crossed the walkway and arrived back to an empty changing room. There was no sign of the supervisor.

He called the elevator and turned to the others. 'Are you five going up or down?'

'Down,' said one of the boys. The others shifted on the spot, looking unsure.

'Me and Jerome are going to the ninth floor. So if you want to go down, you'll need to find another way to do it.'

The girl sat down on the bench beneath the clothes hooks and folded her arms. 'I think we should wait until the supervisor comes back. I don't want to get into trouble.'

Warren rolled his eyes. 'The supervisor isn't coming back. She's busy with whatever's happening up there.' He pointed up. The ceiling shook a second time and Warren thought he heard muffled gunfire.

'What the hell's going on?' said Jerome as though he'd heard the same thing.

Warren shook his head. 'It's got to be rebels.'

Jerome shot him a disbelieving look. 'Why would rebels be in this place? It's an education facility.'

'I'm serious. The voice in the test asked me if there were rebels in Arcis. Why would it ask me that if Arcis wasn't already suspicious?'

'All the more reason to get the hell out of here,' said the girl.

Warren sighed. He couldn't leave. There was nothing left for him back in Oakenfield.

He called the elevator again and waited. There was no stirring of a carriage, no hum of a motor. Nothing.

'Is it broken?' said the boy from Warren's abandoned knife game.

Warren ran a hand through his strawberry-blond hair. 'I don't know. Maybe Arcis has it on lockdown... Crap, I really need to get off this floor.'

'You eager to meet a few rebels?' said Jerome, lifting a brow. 'Because if they're up there like you say, that's what will happen.'

'If it is rebels, they're not here for us. They're here to mess with Arcis. With any luck, the supervisors will take the rebels out and everything will go back to normal. They'll unlock the elevator soon, you'll see.'

'Maybe there's a set of stairs somewhere.' Jerome looked around the room, then back at Warren. 'You know, like an emergency exit in case the elevator is broken?'

Warren clicked his fingers. 'Good thinking.'

They searched the changing room and the adjacent area. All Warren found was solid walls. They found no access point in Tower A, so they agreed to check out Tower B as a group.

'Look how high up we are,' said one of the boys as they hit the walkway again.

Warren crossed fast and avoided looking down. His thoughts shot to Ash and Lilly.

The door to the test area was still unlocked. Warren

ordered everyone to split up. They searched the room but found nothing. Next, they moved to the dining hall, bathrooms and dorm room. There was no sign of an exit point anywhere.

Warren sat on one of the beds in the dorm, his face in his hands. 'There's literally no way off this floor, other than the elevator.'

Jerome sat beside him and patted him on the back. 'Don't worry. The elevator will unlock and we can—'

A loud crash and another vibration nearly knocked Warren to the floor. Jerome jerked back and stared up. The other boys and the girl crouched between two beds.

'What the hell's going on up there?' said Warren.

Jerome continued to stare at the ceiling. 'Beats me, but it's more than just a gunfight.'

Warren stood up. 'I want to check something.'

He returned to the test room and sat in one of the dentist chairs.

Jerome came to his side. 'What are you doing?'

'We can talk to Arcis if we have these circles on our heads. So I thought I'd ask them a few questions.'

Warren hesitated in the chair, worried he might receive another shock.

The screen was blank.

What's happening? What are those noises we keep hearing?

He waited but there was no response.

He tried another chair, another set of circles.

What was that noise? Are there rebels in Arcis?

No response.

It wasn't until the third chair that he finally got an answer.

What's going on? Tell us. The supervisor is gone.

'The ninth floor is under attack. Please stay where

you are. Do not try to leave. Your safety is our utmost priority.'

Attack? From whom?

'The rebels have gained access to our facility and are trying to take it from us.'

The rebels? What do they want?

'We need your cooperation to ensure the rebellion does not destroy the good work Arcis has done here. We are not the enemy.'

Warren needed no convincing of that. He hated the rebels as much as Arcis did. They were trying to destroy the towns' way of life, the status quo. Town life might not suit everyone, but that didn't mean everything should be destroyed.

What can I do to help?

'You can stay here. Don't move. It's for your own safety.'

Give us access to Electro Guns. We can join the fight against them.

'We have the situation under control. Please do not worry.' There was a pause. 'Why do you want to help us?'

Because I hate the rebels and everything about the rebellion.

Another pause. 'I believe you, Warren Hunt. Your heart rate is normal. Were your parents rebels?'

Warren paused.

Yes.

'Why did you lie to us earlier? Tell us where your parents went.'

He yanked the circles from his head before they could shock him again.

'Well, what did Arcis say?' said Jerome.

'It wants us to stay put.'

'So should we?'

The Rebels

The test room gave him the creeps.

'Nah. I'm going to see if I can get the elevator to work.'

Back in the changing room, Warren removed the elevator panel and fiddled around with the components. He had no idea what he was doing, or if he was making things better or worse. But he needed a distraction from what was happening above, and from Arcis' probing questions.

The controllers kept asking about his parents. Who were Philip and Jean Hunt? Were they more than just rebels? Why did Arcis need to know so bad, and in the middle of an attack on its facility?

He replaced the panel and leaned against the wall. The floor rattled again. The vibration felt strongest through the wall; he pulled his back away from it.

Everything went dark as the changing room lights went out.

'I don't like this,' said one of the boys.

Warren stood up and felt his way along the wall to the door between the changing room and the adjoining area. The door was locked.

'Looks like we're stuck here.'

'For how long?' said a panicked Jerome. 'I need to pee.'

'Damn, Jerome. Now I need to go,' said Warren.

'Me too,' said the others.

Warren sat with his legs crossed for what felt like an hour. He eventually relieved himself in one corner. Jerome and the boy did the same.

When the lights finally flickered back on, Warren tried the elevator again. The motor hummed and a noise travelled from the pit below.

His hands sweated as he waited for the elevator to arrive.

There was only one way he was going.

9

The others, scared of being left behind, followed Warren and Jerome into the elevator. The second they did it began to move. With no buttons to select, they rode it up as far as it would take them. The doors opened and Warren stepped out first, into a straight corridor that led to a single door. The corridor was softly illuminated by backlit frosted-glass partitions. Warren walked fast to the door and tried it.

It surprised him to find it unlocked.

A large room awaited that was similar in size to the atrium on the ground floor. Warren walked inside the dark and quiet space, not checking to see if the others had followed. He looked around the windowless room with a half bell-shaped ceiling. The outline of a large machine became clearer, sitting idle in the middle of the room.

Warren hid his relief from the others at having made it to the ninth floor. The truth about his parents' whereabouts had to be hidden in here somewhere.

Small round lights in the machine blinked on and off. As his eyes adjusted more, Warren noticed bodies on the floor. Someone moved, a brown-haired man who looked to be in his early twenties. He was shaking the shoulders of a middle-aged man who sat on the floor with his arms looped around his bended legs.

'Max, come on, we need to go,' said the younger man.

Max didn't respond.

'Hello?' said Warren. He proceeded with caution, aware he might be in the company of rebels. 'What happened here?'

The young man's eyes darted to him and he climbed to his feet. 'Where did you come from?'

'We were trapped on the seventh floor. The elevator took us up.'

The young man narrowed his gaze at him. 'And why the hell would you go up? You need to get out of here. Arcis isn't safe for you. Didn't you hear the gunfire?'

Warren nodded at the man he suspected to be a rebel. 'Yeah. We thought you might need a hand.'

The young man seemed unsure. He looked at Warren, Jerome and the other five.

'Come help me with Max. I need to get him to his feet.'

Warren and Jerome each hooked a hand under Max's armpits.

'She's not here,' muttered Max, as they struggled with his dead weight. 'I thought she'd be here.'

'Come on, Max. Look at me. It's Jason.'

Max stared up at him. 'Where's Preston?'

'He's dead and so are two of the soldiers.'

Max looked dazed as he glanced around. A boy of about fifteen, dressed in a soldier's uniform, was pressed up against one of the walls, staring at the male supervisor. The supervisor seemed frozen into place.

Warren walked over to the soldier. 'What's wrong with the supervisor?'

'They just shut down when the others went through the machine.'

'What do you mean "shut down"?' said Warren.

'I mean, they're not human. They're copies. Check the next room if you don't believe me.'

Jerome and Warren strode to the door located at the back of the room. They found a second identical male supervisor, half in, half out of the room, frozen into place.

With a shiver, Warren opened the door wider and stepped around him. The next room was dark except for dozens of wall units, each with its own faint backlight. He gasped when he saw dozens of male supervisors standing ramrod straight, slotted into the units. Their eyes were open, and all of them stared vacantly ahead.

'What the hell is this?' said Jerome. He walked further into the room and studied one of the supervisors. He poked the supervisor's face. It didn't react.

'Oh, man, they feel so real. Warren, come over here. Touch one, and you'll see what I mean.'

Warren shook his head at a brazen Jerome. He could barely tolerate being in the same room as them, let alone interact with a dead one.

'Nah, you're okay.'

Warren forced himself further inside the room. Now was the perfect time to look for a control room or a console or something—anything that would give him the coordinates to the Beyond.

'Quick,' said Warren. 'Before we have to leave. Help me look for some kind of control panel.'

Jerome did a full lap of the room, while Warren touched whatever he could to see if he could activate something. Apart from the wall units, which had no visible controls, the room was empty.

'Shit.' Warren ran his hands through his hair. 'It has

to be here somewhere.'

Jerome stared at him. 'What do you need the control panel for? Unless you're planning on reactivating these copies?'

'No I wanted to see if we could learn a bit more about Arcis, that's all,' Warren lied. 'The control room for the tests must be on this floor. Maybe it's off the main room.'

Warren hurried back to the main room, and as far from the dead supervisors as possible. There, Jason was helping Max to his feet with the help of the other boys. Jason gripped Max's chin and looked him in the eye. 'Come on, Max. I need your help to get out of here. Anya's gone and we need to find out where she went.'

'Wait,' said Warren. 'What happened to Anya?'

Jason looked at Warren. 'You know my sister?'

His chest tightened. 'You're Anya's brother?' Did he know what Warren had done to Anya? Had she told him before she disappeared? He shook off the thought. 'This is Jerome. We all met on the ground floor.'

Jason stepped forward and shook both of their hands. 'Nice to know she had friends in here.'

Warren discreetly wiped his hand on his trousers. He had just touched a rebel. And that made Anya one too. He was glad they hadn't paired up in the end. But he was still curious about what had happened to her.

'Were there others with her? Dom? Sheila? June? Yasmin?'

Jason nodded.

'What happened to them?'

Jason jerked his head towards the machine in the centre of the room. It had an open tunnel to the front connected to a series of archways inlaid with blinking lights that led to a full-length mirror at the end.

'Arcis forced them to go inside that, and then they disappeared. Arcis stole their memories.'

Warren stared at the machine. 'How?'

'The machine downloaded their memories of their time in Arcis and then forced them to walk through the last arch.'

Both Warren and Jerome moved in for a closer look. The last arch looked like a portal, but he could see through it to the unit at the end.

'Look at this,' said Jerome as he neared the unit.

As Warren got close, he drew in a tight breath. 'What is that?'

He stared at the bottom half of a torso, copied as far as the tops of the legs.

'The final copy didn't take,' said Jason. 'Dom was the last to step through the machine.'

'Hold on one minute.' Warren shook his head. 'Are you saying Anya and Dom stepped through this machine, lost their memories and were copied in the process?'

'That's exactly it,' said Max, standing behind them, sounding more alert. 'Perfect 3D representations of the original design. They're all gone. Both the originals and the copies.'

'Please don't talk about my sister like she's dead,' said Jason.

'We need to face facts, she may well be,' said Max. 'We have no idea what happened to them when they went through that thing.'

Jason shook his head. 'I won't give up looking for her. And you shouldn't give up on your wife until you know for sure what happened to her.'

Max rubbed his chin. 'You're right. I'm sorry. Our priority is getting out of here. Now. The copies may only be temporarily frozen.'

Warren froze at that suggestion. He hadn't finished his search of the room. There had to be a control room that would give him access to Arcis' inner workings. At a minimum, some place from where the tests on the seventh floor were being monitored and controlled. Maybe the tester had catalogued their own thoughts to the answers and left a clue.

'Before we leave, we should check the room. Make sure there isn't some clue as to why Arcis is doing this.'

'We don't have time,' said Max, moving towards the room with the frozen copies.

But Warren ignored him. He ran to the walls, pressed his palms flat against them. He felt no hidden doors. The only door was the one leading to the room with the copies. He continued to run his hands over the panels, concentrating on the space behind the machine. When one of the surfaces clicked, his heart kicked up a notch.

'Over here,' he said, as a secret door exposed a concealed room.

He wanted to go in alone—rebels had no business seeing this—but right now he had to pretend they were all on the same side.

Warren stepped inside what appeared to be a viewing room. He discovered dozens of television screens on one wall, each showing what was happening on the different floors. He recognised the Electro Gun room on the fifth floor and the records room on the first. He searched the cramped space, touching walls and checking for more hidden panels, but there was nothing else but the screens.

He saw the participants on the lower floors, looking dazed and disorientated.

'We need to grab as many of them as possible on the way out,' said Max looking over his shoulder.

'Good idea,' said Jason. 'We should do a sweep through the floors, pick up who we can along the way.'

'There's ten of us,' said Jerome. 'If we take a floor each, more or less, we can be out of here quicker.'

'Agreed,' said Max, picking up guns from the floor and handing them out.

Warren took an Electro Gun and held it close to his chest. He wanted to leave the rebels behind, but without the coordinates for the Beyond, he still needed the rebels to escape Arcis.

'Where are we going?'

'Out of Arcis and Essention then to a safe place in the mountains,' said Max.

Jason stopped. 'No. We need to get to Praesidium. It has to be where Arcis sent Anya. The two places are connected.'

'Soon,' said Max. 'But we'll need food, guns and reinforcements. I won't hit that place with limited weapons and a bunch of drugged-up kids.'

Warren froze at the mention of the rebel mountain stronghold. His parents had told him once about such a place existing, but never mentioned it again. He hadn't placed much value on that information until the day they left him behind. Could his parents have ended up in the stronghold?

If Warren's parents had indeed joined the rebellion fight, then the rebels in the mountain location would know where they'd gone. Perhaps their life lessons weren't bull after all and the Beyond really did exist.

What had Arcis called it? A place beyond the safe zone?

As the rebels prepared to leave, Warren knew his only remaining option was to pretend to be their friend.

10

Warren followed the others through the room with the frozen copies. A stairwell at the far end presented itself and they used it to reach the eighth floor.

He knew there had to be a staircase. He and the others had just combed every inch of Tower B on the seventh floor looking for it, but hadn't uncovered any way to access the upper floors.

'I'll take this floor,' said Max when they reached the eighth. 'The rest of you do a sweep of the other floors and we'll meet in the lobby. You'll have to remove a wall panel when you reach the back of the dorm to access the floor.'

Jason took the seventh while Jerome covered the sixth. Warren took the fifth floor and the others carried on to the lower levels. He entered a corridor that had panels on one side and nothing else. He slid one back until it exposed the dorm room. He passed through the dorm to exit the other side and entered the main room with the combat-maze test in it. There, he carried out a visual search of the floor.

The walls hadn't retracted into the floor. Less than two days ago, Warren had shot at discs using an Electro

The Rebels

Gun in this very room. He avoided entering the maze with the changing walls that could trap him inside. Instead, he called out. One girl and two boys answered and told him they were stuck inside the maze.

'We can't get out!' said the girl.

Warren stood at one entrance to the maze. 'Follow my voice. Use your Electro Guns. Do any of you have shots left?'

'I should have seven shots,' said one boy. 'But our guns stopped working a while ago.'

'The power went down for a bit. Try the guns again.' Warren waited. He heard a discharge of electricity, but it sounded flat.

'It's sparking, that's all. Now what?'

'You'll have to get out the old-fashioned way.' He told them to follow his voice. One by one, they appeared at the entrance, clutching their Electro Guns. They were younger than he was and looked terrified.

'Are there more of you?' he asked.

'No. This is it. What's going on?' One of the boys looked around. 'We were playing the game when the music just stopped. I tried to use my gun but it must've run out of juice.'

'Is there a supervisor around?'

'No, he left when we started playing. He was a bit agitated.'

Warren took an Electro Gun from the girl, pointed it away and fired. The gun stuttered and sparked but emitted no shock. He tried his own. It did the same.

'The lights went out and so did the gun,' said the girl. 'I had at least nine more rounds.'

Warren tossed his gun away; it hit the ground with a thud. He had hoped to take some extra Electro Guns with him, but it appeared the ones in Arcis were tied in to the power. And since everything was down, only conventional guns would do.

'Follow me.'

One of the boys looked confused. 'Where?'

'We're leaving Arcis.'

'We can't. The supervisor said to stay put, not to leave under any circumstances.'

The Compliance in Warren's system dulled his need to focus. But he also felt its hold on him slip due to the fact he hadn't eaten in twelve hours. And because he knew what the drug could do, he could fight against it. For the scared group stood before him, Compliance ruled their actions, thoughts and feelings. Warren would have to work harder to convince them to leave.

'You're going to have to trust me, okay?' said Warren. 'We need to leave. This place isn't safe. The supervisors can't be trusted right now. If you don't come with me, I'm going without you.'

He had no problem leaving them to their fate.

Warren started for the stairwell that lay beyond the dormitory, glancing over his shoulder to check on the others. They followed him like frightened rabbits. Or like lambs to the slaughter—that's how dangerous Compliance could be. For all they knew he could be leading them into a trap. He could have told Max he'd checked the floor and found nothing. His reason for being in Arcis was to get information, not to help Max or Jason. And he'd only used Jerome to get to the ninth floor. What a waste of time that had been because he'd come away empty-handed.

But Max and Jason had already seen people on this floor through the screens on the ninth floor, so he had to return with someone. To get out of Essention, Warren needed to earn both men's trust.

He reached the exposed entrance and entered the

area leading back to the stairwell. As the others followed, his determination to track down his parents increased. All three fifth-floor participants were behind him as he jogged down the stairs.

He stopped at the top of the last set. The stairwell ended one flight below at a door with the number two on it. The only way out would be to cross the second floor walkway and access the elevator on Tower A. If the elevator wasn't working, he might find a set of stairs there. The elevator couldn't be the only way out of this place.

Warren was about to move down the last set of stairs when the door below them opened. The female supervisor entered the stairwell, looking frazzled.

Her expression shifted to anger when she saw them. 'Halt. What are you doing in here?'

Behind him, the others gasped. Warren thought fast. 'There's a problem on the ninth floor. The elevators aren't working. We were told to use the stairs.'

The supervisor's eyes shifted as if she was processing the information. She climbed the stairs until she was on the same level as they were.

'It's against protocol,' she said, twisting her hands together. 'But I can't check or connect to the ninth floor. I don't know what to do.'

'I was just up there,' said Warren. 'Arcis said we should make our way outside where it's safer.' He went to move but the supervisor grabbed his arm.

'Stay there until I can confirm that order.' She pressed a finger to a spot above her ear, activating a tiny silver circle beneath her hair. 'Please confirm the subjects may leave Arcis?'

There was no reply that Warren could hear.

She waited, getting more impatient and irritated. She repeated the request twice more. Warren wondered if the supervisor had the coordinates to the Beyond.

'Please send your instructions.' The supervisor's voice shook. She still had an iron grip on Warren's arm. 'Your humble servant awaits your command, Quintus.'

Her impatience stoked Warren's anxiety. This was his last chance.

Screw it.

'Do you have the coordinates to the Beyond?'

The supervisor turned and gave him an icy stare.

'What did you say?'

He shrank back from her glare and swallowed. 'Nothing. I said nothing.'

In one fluid motion, she spun him around and looped one arm around his middle, locking both arms to his side. He struggled against her restraint, but she was as strong and unyielding as a machine.

He kicked out. 'Let me go!'

'I have a rebel in custody, Quintus. Please advise.'

Warren twisted and grunted, but the supervisor's grip afforded him no room. A loud piercing noise almost deafened him. He was close enough to the supervisor to hear the feedback play through whatever device was attached to the side of her head. She let go and dropped to the floor. His foot caught on the edge of the step and he tumbled down the stairs, landing at the bottom with a thud. The supervisor followed and he rolled out of the way before she could crush him.

He scuttled back, breathing hard at the sight of the lifeless copy that Arcis, or this Quintus person, may have just disabled. He got to his feet. The others stared, visibly shocked by the scene.

Pain bloomed in his arm and he worried it might be broken. He managed to flex his fingers, indicating it was not.

The Rebels

He looked up at the others looking down at him and got to his feet. 'Stop staring and come on. We need to go.'

Warren slipped through the door and left Tower B to cross the walkway. The atrium below was quiet and empty. Mops and buckets lay scattered across the floor. In Tower A, he tried the elevator, but it was offline again. Looking around, he found a final set of stairs in the room adjacent to the changing room that brought them to an area behind the ground-floor dining hall.

He crept out of the hall and into the atrium. Warren jerked to a stop when he saw the shutter to the wolves' cubbyhole was open. Three giant wolves were halfway across the atrium floor, their paws frozen in high mid-step. His eyes never left the unmoving beasts as he passed through the chaotic scene. It looked like the participants had fled in a hurry. The group followed him. When he gave one wolf a final glance he noticed its eyes move. He raced ahead, worried their frozen states were just temporary.

Max, Jason and Jerome waited in the lobby with the others. A group of frightened boys and girls controlled by Compliance huddled together. Max looked relieved to see Warren.

'It's about time,' said Max. 'We were about to leave you behind.'

Warren's expression hardened. *Yeah, story of my life.*

He swallowed his anger and disgust. 'One of the supervisors caught me on the stairs. But I think Arcis might have disabled her. Some kind of feedback played through her communication device before she went limp.'

'Yeah, we saw something similar happen on the third,' said Jason. 'The supervisor there dropped to the floor.'

'I think we should get going,' said Max. 'I don't want to be here when those wolves in the atrium wake up.'

They all agreed, including the frightened lambs most affected by Compliance.

Warren followed Max and Jason out of Arcis, towards the perimeter, to the force field. Warren, Jerome and the others had the right chips that would get them through the force field. But Jason, Max and the soldier might not be so lucky.

But Max walked right through without any problems.

'The force field is down,' he said. 'Quickly. Before this place resets itself.'

It was early morning and the sun was rising in the east. Not a soul was out on the streets.

A deep rumbling sounded beyond Essention's walls.

'What the hell is that?' said Jerome.

Jason sprinted to the nearby Monorail station and climbed the stairs to the platform. He scaled a safety railing and held on to a vertical pole for support as he looked over Essention's perimeter wall in the distance. He gasped then climbed back down.

'Hovering transporters are coming this way. Giant diggers. Large claw mechanisms. I can see the plumes of dust swirling in the distance. They're approaching at a steady pace. It won't be long before they're here.'

'How long?' said Max.

'Maybe twenty minutes.'

'What do they want?' said Warren.

'They're coming to break apart Essention,' said Max. 'We need to get everyone out.'

11

The commotion outside Essention woke up the residents in several houses. Lights flicked on and faces appeared at windows. Some wandered outside to take a look.

When their group of ten reached East Essention, where the orphans had been housed, Max told everyone to begin knocking on doors. Frightened boys and girls answered their doors.

'You need to leave Essention,' said Warren, when a girl gave him a blank look.

'Why?'

'Because giant machines are coming to break the urbano apart and you shouldn't be here.'

The girl's eyes widened. 'But... Essention is my home now. I have nowhere else to go.'

'I don't have time to argue. There are others who need our help.' Warren sighed. 'Look, are you coming or not?'

The girl bit her lip and looked around, unsure.

Warren walked away. 'Fine. Suit yourself. I have to go.'

He met up with the others after they'd finished their house calls. Other orphans had joined the group which was now thirty strong. Warren didn't bother checking to see if the girl he'd spoken to was with them. His survival was his number one priority now.

'This is taking too long, Max,' said Jason.

'I agree. We need a better way to tell everyone. Come on. Let's find Charlie. If he can hack in to the communication system, we'll be able to cover more ground.'

Max led them to a gate behind a block of apartments in East. There was a strip of overgrown land behind the houses. 'This way. It's blocked in parts, so we'll have to climb over. But it's the shortest route to Southwest.'

Max opened the gate and ushered everyone inside. Warren pushed ahead of the orphans who were still on Compliance and moving slower than him. Jason took the lead while Max brought up the rear. They exited at the entrance to Essention and close to the hospital.

The hospital block with the see-through walls was plunged into darkness, but Warren saw people moving about inside. Jason opened another gate connecting to a strip of land behind the houses in Southwest where the land was better kept and easier to navigate.

After a short distance, Jason stopped at a seven-foot wall covered by bushes to the rear of the houses in Southwest. Max joined him and together they pulled back the bush to reveal a hole in the wall. Warren made sure to squeeze in ahead of the others. On the other side, Max opened the back door to a house and ushered them all in.

An old man appeared at the kitchen door, wrench in hand. He held it like a weapon.

'Where the hell have you been? Did you hear that racket outside?'

'It's the Praesidium machines, Charlie,' said Jason. 'They're coming with diggers. They're going to rip this place apart.'

Charlie nodded. 'Reinforcements arrived while you were in Arcis. How did it go? Did you find her?'

'Another time, Dad,' said Max. 'We'll talk when we're out of here safely.'

'Right, yes. We should all get moving.'

Charlie turned to leave but Max stopped him. 'Not yet. The urbano is full of disorientated and compliant kids. We need to warn them, but we're too slow on foot. Can you hack the communication system wired into the houses, get a message out?'

'That would be even slower. We wouldn't have enough time. But I have another idea.' Charlie left the room and returned with a megaphone. 'Will this do? We'll need to get higher. It won't reach everyone, but it's the best we can hope for.'

Max nodded and took it from him.

Warren followed Max upstairs and watched as he climbed out of a window onto the roof. The megaphone squealed when he turned it on. Max brought it to his lips.

'People of Essention. You need to leave your homes. You are no longer safe here. Praesidium has sent machines to tear this urbano apart. If you don't believe me, look out your window and you will see the dust the machines are kicking up beyond the walls. They will arrive shortly. Take nothing and run to the exit.'

Max climbed back in the window and threw the megaphone on the bed.

'We need to collect everything we brought. Warren, please help Charlie.'

The bungalow was close enough to Essention's exit that Warren could leave without Max and the others. But he had no idea where to go, where would be safe. At least the rebels could guarantee his safety on the outside.

He nodded and found Charlie in the living room, instructing the group to carry guns and equipment. Jason was emptying the contents of a hidden storage area into a bag. Charlie handed Warren and Jerome an empty rucksack each and told them to pack food from the kitchen. He kept a third bag in hand.

'Do you think the residents will leave?' said Jerome to Charlie as he stuffed cans and cutlery into the bag.

'I don't know, son,' said Charlie, filling his pack. 'All I know is we need to get out of here before this place reboots itself. If that happens, we'll have more pressing worries than those diggers out there.'

'Like what?' said Jerome.

'Like getting past the disintegration guns monitoring the outside, for one. While this place is offline, we have a shot. I don't know if the guns will power up, but if they do, we won't make it five feet past those walls.'

They gathered what they could and everyone met outside in the back garden. After squeezing through the hole in the wall, they ran along the strip of land for Essention's exit.

Warren looked at the hospital again. Patients had hands and faces pressed up against the windows, looking confused. Some were banging on the glass. The place appeared to be on lockdown. He wondered if they'd heard Max's warning. Some figures inside the hospital were frozen in place. Copies, he presumed.

The shiny orbs that normally patrolled close to the hospital were nowhere in sight. The group made it to the gate without any trouble.

Max pulled on the gate and it moved a little. 'It's on manual lockdown only. We should be able to open it.'

Warren and Jerome helped Max pull it back far enough for the others to squeeze through. They gathered on the other side of the gate, but stopped when Max put his hand up.

'Don't go any further. I'll need to check the guns.'

He approached the lip of the brick facade that was part of the recessed entrance. Warren saw him look up then pull back.

'No. This isn't going to work.' Max backtracked to Essention's main gate.

'What's the matter?' asked Charlie.

'The guns. They're active. Moving slowly, but still moving. We'd be ripped apart before we reached safety outside of their sensors.'

'So what do we do now?' said Warren.

Charlie's eyes brightened. 'The tunnel. We can use it to escape.'

'How?' said Max. 'You collapsed it. Digging it out would take too long.'

They moved back to the strip of land behind Southwest.

Charlie shook his head. 'I never collapsed it. I just covered it up.'

'Jesus, Dad. That was risky. What if they'd found it?'

'A risk worth taking, I'd say, given our present predicament.'

The noise beyond Essention's perimeter grew louder.

'They're about a mile out,' said Max. 'I saw them while I was checking the guns. We need to go. I don't think they'll bother with the main entrance. More likely, they'll hit the side of the urbano.'

Warren heard a hissing noise. He looked around. A thick gas drifted up through the grates in the ground. The revolting smell forced him to pinch the end of his nose.

'What's that?'

'Arcis is gassing the urbano,' said Jason, breathing into his sleeve. 'We need to get out of here.'

'Everyone, cover your mouths,' said Charlie.

The group ran back to Charlie's house. Everywhere, the gas leaked out of hidden grates. They coughed and spluttered as they tried to run while holding their breath. Some dropped, and Jerome went to help them.

'Leave them,' Max warned.

Warren's eyes watered and stung as the gas reached him. He coughed and pulled his T-shirt up high to cover his mouth and nose. The others did the same with their clothing. Both Charlie and Max held the cloth bags to their faces. They lunged for the hole in the wall and groped for the back door.

Inside the house, Warren gasped and sucked in new air. They'd lost three people; all orphans on Compliance who hadn't reacted fast enough.

He followed Charlie into the basement. There, he saw a false wall and mounds of dirt piled up in one corner of the room. Charlie, Max, Jason, Jerome and the soldier dismantled the false wall that covered a large tunnel.

'Inside, quickly,' said Charlie.

Warren turned to see the gas leaking through the air vents in the ceiling. The whole building was rigged.

A prickle hit his lungs and he lunged for the tunnel. The low ceiling forced him onto all fours. He moved as fast as he could. The boy in front was too slow. Panic rose in Warren's throat when he smelled the noxious gas at the start of the tunnel.

'Hurry up!' he shouted at the boy, who picked up the pace a little.

Warren's throat pinched and his eyes stung.

The tunnel veered upwards and Warren clambered

out of the hole onto a grassy area outside of Essention. They all ran for the tree line in the distance. When they reached safety, Warren looked back at Essention.

Max had been right. Through teary eyes, he watched the diggers break through one of the side walls. Screams filled the air. He thought of all the people who had refused to leave. They should have heeded Max's warning. He tried not to think about the patients trapped in the hospital.

Minutes passed and one of the machines emerged from the large gaping hole in the side of Essention. It carried a pile of bodies on its flat bed. It tipped the bed and dropped the bodies onto the grass.

Warren turned away, sickened. Had the rebels also acted without remorse when they'd carried out their raids on the towns in the name of freedom?

Their group, led by Max and Jason, trekked silently through the trees. The burn in Warren's throat and nose lessened. They entered a clearing and a town came into view: Glenvale.

Max coughed into his fist as they approached it. 'We need to pack everything and get going.'

Warren tensed up at the sight of snipers on the tops of the walls. Scanners perched up high bathed them in a blue light as they waited at the entrance.

The gates to Glenvale opened and Warren absorbed the layout of the town that acted as some kind of operational base. Floodlights brightened the main streets. There was even an armoury that soldiers, dressed in green garb, were in the process of dismantling.

A female soldier in her early twenties approached Max. 'The minute we saw the machines coming for Essention we started to pack up.'

Ten minutes later, the trucks parked inside Glenvale were full and ready to go. Warren and Jerome climbed inside a truck with Max and Charlie.

'Where are we going?' said Warren.

'To a safe haven in the mountains. It's too risky to stay here now. Praesidium will be looking for us. The controllers will know we've escaped Arcis. The rest of our people are at the safe haven. It's a place the machines don't know about.'

Warren's pulse thrummed. Would he find his parents there?

He gripped the underside of his seat as the truck pulled out of Glenvale, heading away from Ession.

What if there was no Beyond, like Arcis had assumed there was? What if his parents had made it up to get rid of him?

12

The vehicle bumped along the road that led to the mysterious mountain stronghold. The driver had cranked up the speed to outrun any machine that might follow.

Warren tried not to think about the bodies he'd seen outside Essention, or how many more the machines had added to the pile since they left. What if the tunnel hadn't been available? So many people gassed. So many people discarded like waste. How could Praesidium allow that to happen?

'Praesidium built both Essention and Arcis,' Max had said when the truck first moved off. 'They put machines in charge of both places. Praesidium is most likely retrieving the technology. That's why the machines are tearing Essention apart. Everyone living inside the walls is expendable.'

The thought turned Warren's stomach. Being on the side of the rebels didn't seem like such a bad idea.

He wondered about Anya and June, even Dom and Sheila. What had happened to them? Where had they gone? Had they been sent to Praesidium? Seeing Dom's half-copied legs inside the machine on the ninth floor had opened up new questions: one being, why they had been copied at all.

He recalled his parents' last conversation with him, the night before they'd left. His mother had made his favourite for dinner: chicken and roast potatoes. If Warren had been paying attention, he would have realised it was their last supper together. But nothing about that night had seemed out of place.

His father had been reading Praesidium's latest news article using a handheld computer.

'It says here Praesidium is giving the towns new growth-promoting lights for the vertical farms,' he said.

'Well that's good news,' said his mother.

'Increases the growth by at least three times what we have now.' He scrolled down the page. 'Possibly as soon as three months, Praesidium says.'

His mother smiled sadly. 'Just in time for spring.'

'Crops and food supplies are low now. We needed it three months ago.'

'Dad, what's Praesidium like?' said Warren.

His father looked up. 'The city? It has all the latest technology. The towns survive off their scraps.'

Warren pointed to the computer in his father's hand. 'But we have tech here.'

He waved the object at him. 'Tech rejects, son. That's why we need electronics experts and engineers and code writers in the towns. So we can fix the junk they give us.'

Jean set the food down on the table. 'Put it away, Philip. Time to eat.'

They sat at the table. Warren scooted his chair in. 'What about the vertical farms? I mean, isn't that a Praesidium idea? Isn't that the city passing on their better tech to us?'

His father gave a short laugh. 'Vertical farms have

been around for a long time. In fact, I think it was Hal Trudeau over in Glenvale who came up with the concept. The tech we use to increase the growing time is from Praesidium. But it's still too slow. I'm certain the city perfected growth acceleration by a factor of three several years ago.'

'So why wait so long to give it to us?'

'Because the city wants us to be independent. But I think it's because it wants us to fail.'

'I don't think Praesidium is like that, Dad. It's been good to us.'

Warren saw his mother shake her head softly at his father.

Nobody talked much over dinner. Jean cleared the dishes and whispered something to Philip. She gave Warren a soft smile then left the room once the kitchen was back in order. His father went to bed.

She returned a few minutes later and handed Warren some cash. 'Your father and I need to go out tomorrow, so can you pick up some things while we're gone? I'll leave a note on the table for you when you get up. Be sure to check the table when you wake, okay?'

'Sure,' said Warren. She kissed him and hurried off to bed.

Warren had found the note his mother had promised to leave all right. But it wasn't a shopping list...

The truck travelled along a bumpy section of the road, jolting Warren out of his thoughts. His head banged off the side of the truck and he released a curse. Jerome sat opposite him, fast asleep, with Max on one side and Charlie on the other. Jason was to Warren's left. Warren shook his head at Jerome's ability to sleep through most anything. He'd always been the first to fall asleep in Arcis.

Warren held on tighter as the road got bumpier.

'We're almost there,' said Max. 'We need to cross some rough terrain to get to the entrance of the safe haven. The machines have difficulty navigating the valley area.'

Warren could see nothing out of the windowless truck.

The vehicle came to a stop.

'Okay, everyone out,' said Max. 'This is as far as the trucks can go. Grab the bags you brought.'

It was dark when they climbed out. They walked for about a mile along a narrow path and arrived at a large, gated compound. Warren waited with his food bag while a blue scanner, similar to the one at Glenvale, checked the entire group.

Men and women dressed in fatigues and carrying weapons arrived and stood in front of them. One with a handheld computer stepped forward and showed it to Max.

Max's face darkened. 'Take the Arcis teens to the holding cells.'

'Are you sure?' said Charlie. 'They've already been through enough.'

'I'm sure.' Max showed Charlie the computer and Charlie let out a soft curse.

'How did we miss it?'

'Probably because the tech was offline,' said Max.

'Did the controllers at Arcis know?'

Max turned to the group of Arcis participants and said, 'The scanner is identifying one of you as a Praesidium copy. Identify yourself or you all risk being detained indefinitely at this facility.'

Warren looked around at the group of ten. Jerome shrugged at him.

'Okay, have it your way. You will all be detained for questioning.'

The Rebels

A rebel soldier grabbed Warren's arm and led him through the gates. He took him to a large building set against a mountainous backdrop. Inside, the soldier dumped him in one of several rooms along a corridor.

'Wait. I'm not a copy. I think I'd know if I were one.'

The soldier closed the door without reply. Warren heard him pacing outside the room. He sat on the bed and leaned forward. Why would the rebels even think there was a copy from Praesidium? What did that even mean?

Maybe this was a test, to weed out those disloyal to the cause. He'd failed his parents' test during their last dinner. They'd painted Praesidium in a bad light— possibly on purpose—and Warren had defended the city. That's why they'd abandoned him.

He rested his head against the wall.

Had his parents really come through this rebel mountain stronghold? Had they betrayed the rebels here? He was terrified to ask. By revealing who he was, who his parent were, Warren could be walking into a trap.

This could be the rebels' attempts to break him. To trick him into revealing the contents of the note that mentioned the Beyond.

$$\Omega$$

An hour later, the door opened and Max walked in. From his position on the bed, Warren watched as Max dragged a chair over and sat down in front of him.

'I've chatted with some of the others. Charlie is talking to the rest. You know why you're here?'

'Yeah, because you think I'm a copy. You know that's stupid, right?'

'I need to know where you came from.'

Warren tensed up, reminded of the questions in Arcis and the punishment.

'Oakenfield.'

'What did your parents do there?'

'My father was a farmer and my mother was a teacher.' It was the truth as he knew it.

'And can anyone vouch for that?'

'No. I mean, anyone who came from Oakenfield can. But I didn't meet anyone from my town, except for Tahlia.'

'And is Tahlia here?'

'No. She's dead.'

'So how did you end up in Arcis? What happened to your parents?'

He told Max he'd been in the house alone when the rebels had attacked Oakenfield. When he got sick, people from Praesidium had rescued him. He left out the part about his parents' abandoning him.

Max nodded. 'That seems to fit the general story around here. So what can you tell us about Jerome?'

'Jerome? He's a friend. We started in Arcis at the same time. Why?'

'And he doesn't have parents, is that right?'

'He's an orphan, if that's what you mean.' Warren scrubbed his head trying to remember more. 'I think Jerome lived with a boy called Frank and his uncle, before his uncle was killed.'

Warren pulled his legs up to his chest. 'Why are you keeping me here? I'm not a copy, I swear.'

Max stood up. 'We know you're not. But we think your friend Jerome might be.'

Ω

Max released Warren a short time later. One of the soldiers escorted him to the main accommodation area, then left. Warren stayed outside the block for a moment and looked around. From what he could see of the poorly lit compound, the safe haven was larger than Oakenfield. Dim lights stretched into the distance. Looming shadows of the mountain pass on either side watched over the rebel base. Faint outlines of people became clear, positioned up high on what looked like a mountain road or ledge.

Charlie joined him and pointed up to the mountain ridge.

'See up there?' Warren nodded, seeing the glints of light. 'They're our spotters. They're monitoring the area out there and above us, making sure we don't get any nasty surprises. Like the flying orbs.'

'What about the machines?'

'They can't get inside the valley. We use anti-magnetic fields. Where the trucks dropped us off was outside of the range. Our driver reported a low level of resistance even before we reached the edge of the field. It was because of Jerome.'

'What will happen to him?'

Charlie walked on. 'Come with me.'

Warren hesitated a moment before following him through the compound.

'This place hid the first band of rebels who separated from the towns,' the old man said.

Warren's pulse thundered in his ears. He wanted to ask Charlie if his parents were here. But despite Charlie's friendly disposition, something stopped him.

The old man continued. 'This place was designed to be temporary. We had hoped to convince enough of the townspeople to join us here, to make a new life outside of Praesidium's control. But many didn't trust our motives.

So we fully separated from the towns, made this compound more permanent.'

'Does everyone from the towns come here first?'

'Yes, but some move on.'

'How old are the people who come here?' Warren waited, nervous to hear Charlie's reply.

'Mostly young men and women. An older couple passed through here about six months ago, but they didn't stay. There were rumours they made it to the Beyond.'

Warren could barely breathe. 'The Beyond?'

'The place where many believe we came from. We've never seen it, or know if it exists.'

'How do you know if they made it to there? The couple, I mean.'

'Like I said, rumours. Two witnesses swear they saw them pass through. But we haven't been able to verify the Beyond's location.' Charlie watched him. 'Have you ever heard of such a place?'

Warren shook his head.

'Were your parents murdered before you became sick, before Praesidium rescued you?'

Warren almost blurted out the truth. That he believed his parents were the couple who had passed through. But Charlie was fishing for something. He could see it in his eyes. Warren wasn't sure if he could trust him.

He shook his head.

Charlie patted him on the back. 'It will get easier to talk about. Come on. I want to show you the rest of the place.'

The compound was surrounded by a large, thick wall with metal gates that were opened manually.

'We don't use technology here because the machines can hack into it. The compound is separated into several areas: training room, tech room, kitchen, accommodation. There's even a barber shop.'

'A barber shop? Why?' The only barber shop Warren knew about was in Glenvale.

Charlie laughed. 'To give us a sense of normality. We do it because it's a human thing to care about your hair. It gives us our individuality.' He pointed to Warren's longish strawberry-blond hair. 'Who cut yours last?'

'I did.'

'Well it looks like you hacked at it with blunt scissors.'

Warren blushed. 'I did.'

'I'm a barber by trade, so when you get settled in, I want you to come see me. My shop is just over there.' He pointed to a street with what looked like a few trading premises.

Some soldiers approached Charlie and greeted him with warm hugs.

'I've been dying for you to get back,' said a smiling male soldier in his early twenties. 'My hair's a total disaster.'

Charlie laughed. 'Come see me tomorrow and I'll get it sorted for you.'

The soldier nodded and walked on.

As they continued their tour, Warren thought about one of the questions Arcis had asked him. 'Is this a safe zone?'

'Yeah, you could call it that. It's outside of Praesidium's range of detection. The mountains block their signals. Plus we have other equipment that prevents them from seeing us.'

'So what happens now?'

Charlie walked on, hands behind his back. 'Now we figure out how to get the others back—the ones who made it to the ninth floor and were sent from Arcis to

Praesidium.'

Anya, June, Sheila, Dom, Yasmin.

'And Jerome?'

'He stays put until we can determine if he's linked to Praesidium or operating on his own. It was a massive risk bringing him here.'

'If it helps, I don't think he knows what he is.'

Charlie nodded. 'I believe you, but try convincing my son. Now, go get some rest. We have a lot of work to do tomorrow.'

Warren headed for the accommodation block, believing now that his parents had come through this place. He still had no idea why Charlie had quizzed him about the Beyond. Did he know who his parents were? Were Philip and Jean Hunt the only tangible link to its existence?

If the information wasn't in Arcis, how had his parents located it? Perhaps the coordinates were hidden in Praesidium?

Warren found a free bed and lay down on it. He draped an arm over his eyes and made a decision: to help the rebels gain access to Praesidium.

Then, when he made it inside the city, he would steal the coordinates to the Beyond and get the hell out of here.

Ω
Continue the series

The Collective (Book 2)
The Haven (Book 3)
The Beyond (Book 4)

The Rebels

Other Books by Eliza Green
Genesis Series

GENESIS CODE

An alien hunter is caught in a dangerous game of cat and mouse.

Investigator Bill Taggart will stop at nothing to find his missing wife. But standing between him and the truth is a secretive alien species on a distant planet. When his government pushes him to observe the species ahead of plans to relocate Earth's population, Bill crashes straight into the path of one alien.

The surprising confrontation forces Bill to question whether the investigation into the savage species is needed. But when official government intel disagrees with the cold hard facts, he worries there might be another reason for the relocation plans.

A snap government order leaves the investigator in limbo and facing off against a new enemy that is more dangerous than the first. Worse, this enemy appears to live close to home.

A devastating set of plans is soon revealed that will destroy the lives on two worlds. And Bill is caught in the middle. Can he stop chasing ghosts long enough to save humanity from the real enemy?

Get *Genesis Code*

Available in Digital and Paperback

www.elizagreenbooks.com/genesis-code

Genesis (Book 0) Get this teaser story for free only when you sign up to my mailing list. Check out **www.elizagreenbooks.com** for more information.

Duality (Standalone)

Jonathan Farrell is stuck between two realities. Who put him there, and can he escape before he loses his grip on the real world? Read this story with flavours of *The Matrix* and *Inception*.

www.elizagreenbooks.com/duality

BOOKS BY KATE GELLAR

Eliza also writes paranormal romance under the pen name, Kate Gellar.

The Irish Rogue Series begins with *Magic Destiny*.

Book 1: One novice witch must temper her conflicting magic before the wrong one unleashes a new power nobody can stop.

Available in both digital and paperback from Amazon.

Rogue Magic (a free prequel to *Magic Destiny* when you sign up to my mailing list. Check out **www.kategellarbooks.com** for more information)

Reviews

Word of mouth is crucial for authors. If you enjoyed this book, please consider leaving a review where you purchased it; make it as long or as short as you like. I know review writing can be a hassle, but it's the most effective way to let others know what you thought. Plus, it helps me reach new readers instantly!

Get in Touch

www.twitter.com/elizagreenbooks
www.facebook.com/elizagreenbooks
www.instagram.com/elizagreenbooks
www.wattpad.com/elizagreenbooks
Goodreads – search for Eliza Green

Printed in Great Britain
by Amazon